Dr. Id-entity,

OR,

Farewell to Plaquedemia,

A

PULP SCIENCE FICTION NOVEL.

Book One of the Scikungfi Trilogy

THE FIRST EDITION

Edited by Dr. Master Master Stanley Ashenbach Esquire

HYATTSVILLE:
Printed by RAW DOG SCREAMING PRESS in Maryland,
and for STICK FIGURE INCORPORATED in
Pseudofolliculitis City.

MMVII.

RAW DOG
SCREAMING
PRESS

other books by d. harlan wilson

The Kafka Effekt
Stranger on the Loose
Pseudo-City

Published by Raw Dog Screaming Press,
Hyattsville, MD

First Paperback Edition

Cover image: Morten Bak
Book design: Jennifer Barnes

Printed in the United States of America

ISBN 978-1-933293-32-5

Library of Congress Control Number: 2006938877

www.rawdogscreaming.com

acclaim for d. harlan wilson & dr. identity

———

"D. Harlan Wilson is my favorite author. His books are really great!"
Franz Kafka

"Amazing. Brilliant. *Dr. Identity* blew me away."
Walter Cronkite

"Postmodernism is dead. D. Harlan Wilson is alive."
Fredric Jameson

"Science fiction this gripping is a rare thing. Think Quentin Tarantino
meets Isaac Asimov. Think William Gibson meets Jorge Luis Borges. Think
the Macho Man Randy Savage body slams George Orwell. In this gritty,
gruesome technoir, Wilson depicts an imploded world in which humanity has
succumbed to the mistress of technology: people willfully replace themselves
with androids on a daily basis, jetpacks and propeller beanies are the dominant
mode of transportation, members of the 'Papanazi' are more numerous than
businessmen, and ultraviolent 'scikungfi' fights materialize on every seedy
street corner and flyway. *Dr. Identity* is the next evolutionary stage in literature.
A dangerous read in every way."
The Boston Post

"Breathtaking prose. Wilson is the real deal. And he's not even gay!"
Gertrude Stein

"Breathtaking prose. Wilson is the real deal. And he's not even gay!"
Ernest Hemingway

"I wish I could write fiction like that fuckin' D. Harlan Wilson!"
Vladimir Nabokov

"Dr. Wilson is a plaquedemic to be reckoned with. His writing will kick your ass and take your name—Agent Smith style."
Hugo Weaving

"Oui oui!"
The Paris Review

"There's 99.9% of the science fiction genre, and there's D. Harlan Wilson."
Amazing Stories

"Wilson is an episteme in and of himself. History is history because he says so."
Michel Foucault

"*Dr. Identity* is an original book with a unique plot and lots of suspense."
Condoleezza Rice

"This novel is too mindblowing, too inconceivable, too utterly *perfect* to actually exist. I don't believe in this novel, and you can't make me."
Norman Mailer

"In Wilson, the twenty-first century has found its first and last authentic voice."
Fortnightly Review

"I can't say enough about this book! I laughed all the way through it! Ha! I don't really understand it. It doesn't go in a straight line, as it were. It has no discernable purpose and the characters are as flat as manholes. But it's so goddamn funny! Ha!"
Fyodor Dostoevsky

"Is D. Harlan Wilson a cartoon?"
Philip K. Dick

"D. Harlan Wilson is Philip K. Dick's ghost."
Horselover Fat

"Monstrous. Beautiful."
Newsweek

"If I have another party, I'm asking D. Harlan Wilson to buy the flowers."
Virginia Woolf

"*Dr. Identity* is like my chicken: fingerlickin' good."
Colonel Sanders

"Badass."
Lance Henriksen

"The most important book of the twenty-first century. Probably the most important book ever written. *Dr. Identity* reaches new literary heights. A truly remarkable work written by a bona fide genius."
The Daily Standard

"My son is talented and artistic and smart and a marvelous teacher!"
D. Harlan Wilson's Mom

"What can I say? *Dr. Identity* is what happens when you do it like Big Daddy Wilson."
Jacques Derrida

"If I weren't me, I'd want to be D. Harlan Wilson."
Igsnay Bürdd

"Quick-witted, misogynistic *commedia del foul* at its best."
James Fenimore Cooper

"D. Harlan Wilson is very tall. He's like six and a half feet tall!"
Kathy Acker

"A narratological feat of strength."
Nickelodeon

"Scientifiction of the utmost caliber."
John W. Campbell

"D. Harlan's kiss is on my list."
Daryl Hall

"Not an Oprah book."
Oprah Winfrey

"Professor Wilson is a big fan of my musicals. He always talks about me. Last year he taught *Cats* in a LACT (Literature about Creatures with Tails) course. He sends me postcards all the time. Once he sent me a singing telegram for my birthday. How bad could his writing be?"
Andrew Lloyd Weber

"Enter the quixotic cityscape of Bliptown, home to a nameless English professor and his psychotic mechanical sidekick. Following the accidental murder of a student, the 'Dystopian Duo,' as the media calls them, set out on a dazzling journey to the end of the night…Nothing is taboo here. Taboo is a normative condition, in fact. And yet *Dr. Identity* is among the classiest, most sophisticated works ever written—at once a cult favorite and a canonical jewel."
Le Figaro

"No one writes gooder than D.!"
John Steinbeck

"Wilson's Puerto Rican roots really come out in his debut novel. An elegiac and moving storyteller, he has a real genius for the material of personal experience…Unforgettable, rich and lively."
Vogue

"D. Harlan Wilson's prose can cut tin cans in half."
Grover Cleveland

"*Dr. Identity* deserves to be read aloud by me. This book and my larynx were born for one another."
Charlton Heston

"I have to admit, next to this remarkable novel, *Invisible Man* looks like a Harlequin Romance."
Ralph Ellison

"Dr. Identity is the chicest, manliest character to hit the bookshelves since Jane Austen's Mr. Darcy."
Las Vegas Weekly

"Yo D.!"
Fritz Lang

"D. Harlan Wilson is a sentient exclamation point."
Stanley Ashenbach

"The special effects in this book put films like *The Matrix* and its successors to shame. Eat your heart out Keanu! Sometimes the action seems a bit too choreographed for its own good, but that's a small price to pay for this stunning *tour de force* of contemporary bookmaking. *Dr. Identity* deserves a catalog of sequels the likes of the *Friday the 13th* series. Other Winter blockbusters will shrink in comparison. Wilson cleverly pulls back curtain after curtain only to expose another curtain. His novel is kinetic, atmospheric, moody, dark, creamy, and downright hilarious (not to mention elaborately plotted, androgynously gorgeous, and brilliantly realized). Finally a piece of literature that delivers."
Curious George Journal

"A gold-plated toilet bowl of sci-fi meatloaf."
Meatloaf

"Unrelenting suspense. Unabashed foresight."
The Teufelsdröckh Review

"The future is *Dr. Identity*."
Alfred Bester

"Pussies don't read D. Harlan Wilson."
Gary Busey

"Sensational and singularly convincing."
Fantastic Story Quarterly

"Wow. This is some book."
Thomas Pynchon

"A real edge-of-your-seat page-turner…Stark and gripping…Absorbing…Chilling…Complex and convincing…Awe-inspiring…[Wilson] brings the food to the table and eats it all himself…Relentlessly intense. Kung fu (not to mention Asian culture in general) will never be the same…Ignites like a

flamethrower, burns like a forest fire…Impossible to put down…A terrific read…Compassionate, superbly [argued,] [fluidly written…Fascinating]… Original…More fun than a pocket full of dynamite."
Life Magazine

"I like his verbs. His nouns and prepositions are ok. But his verbs are straight outta Schoolhouse Rock!"
Fifth Grade Student

"Few authors have the ability to deploy gerunds with the skill and precision of D. Harlan Wilson."
William Strunk, Jr.

"Wilson is a scumbag, and his new novel—I won't even say its name—is basically a fictionalized version of *Mein Kampf*. This author is a menace and a shiteating pimp. Given the opportunity I would rip out his Adam's apple and piss on his corpse. If ever a book should be burned, this is the one."
Anne Coulter

"Murder achieves new heights in *Dr. Identity*. At last, here is a piece of literature that articulates the prickly art of death-dealing with a sense of style. Ha ha ha goes Saucy Jack."
Jack the Ripper

"*Dr. Identity* is like the sound of a million cow bells going *dink-dink-dink* in the sky."
Christopher Walken

"In the wake of *Dr. Identity*, capitalist schiz-flows will never be the same."
Gilles Deleuze & Félix Guattari

"Hiyaaaaaaaaaaaaaaaaaaaaaaaaaaaaaaaaaah!!!"
Bruce Lee

"Hiyaaaaaaaaaaaaaaaaaaaaaaaaaaaaaaaaaah!!!"
Howard Dean

"Kaaaaaaaaaaaaaaaaaaaaaaaaaaaaaaaaaaahn!!!"
James T. Kirk

"To be the man, you gotta beat the man. Wooooh!!!"
Ric Flair

"Naw mean?"
Custodian at Stick Figure University

"A handsome read."
Calvin Klein

"Someday people will look back at the twenty-first century and say: 'That was the era of *Dr. Identity*.'"
Pall Mall Gazette

"D. Harlan Wilson writes voodoo architecture of the soul."
Frank Lloyd Wright

"D. Harlan Wilson is the kind of motherfucking Yankee you want on your team."
William Faulkner

"D. Harlan Wilson's fiction is the equivalent of the Bee Gees Greatest Hits on steroids."
Scientific Amerikan

"At the core of this thrilling tale is a revelation of the (post)human condition. [Wilson] exposes the gruesome underbelly of a dystopia shaped by absurdist laws, madcap ideologies and technologized desires. *Dr. Identity* represents the nightmare of reason. It satirizes the machinery of existence. It poses as a tightly clenched sphincter with glitter sprinkled on top. This book doesn't have teeth. It has fangs, and if you bite it, it will bite you back."
Tyra Banks

––––––––

For Stanley, who died in Venice

TABLE OF CONTENTS

identity *n.* **2.** The set of behavioral or personal traits by which an individual is recognizable as a member of a group. **3.** The quality or condition of being the same as something else.

plaque *n.* **3.b.** A deposit of fatty material on the inner lining of the arterial wall, characteristic of atherosclerosis. **c.** A scaly patch formed on the skin by psoriasis. **d.** A film of mucous and bacteria on the tooth surface.

academic *adj.* **4.** Scholarly to the point of being unaware of the outside world. **8.** Having no practical purpose or use.

—American Heritage College Dictionary

00
dostoevsky & lucille – 1st person ('blah)

I returned from the meeting with the chair of the department feeling embittered and hostile. The topic of discussion had been plastic forks. It wasn't the topic's first appearance. As always, I was blamed for the "unreasonably swift" depletion of the department's supply. The reason? Gilbert Hemingway once caught me removing two forks from the utensil drawer.

"Fork hog," he muttered, spying on me from down the hallway.

I squinted at him. "Excuse me?"

His square, bearded head angled out of his office door. The head disappeared from view as if yanked by a string and the door slammed shut.

He confronted me about the issue later that afternoon in the men's room. I was halfway finished with my business when he sidled up to the urinal next to me.

"I saw you," he whispered, raising a bristly eyebrow.

I squinted at him. "Excuse me?"

He refused to believe me when I told him that the additional fork was for my officemate. After that, whenever the supply of forks went dry, he called me into his office and reprimanded me in various passive-aggressive ways. Sometimes he questioned my motives. Sometimes he insulted my character. Sometimes he threatened to cut utensil funding so as to force me to bring my own tackle into work. He never raised his voice or gesticulated in any way; he was invariably calm and pragmatic. Today, however, he threw a half-eaten plum at me. I was a relatively new assistant professor who had a long way to go before securing tenure. The gesture worried me.

I returned to my office to find Bob Dostoevsky blowdrying his armpits. Like Gilbert Hemingway and the rest of the faculty employed by Corndog University's English department, Bob had legally changed his surname to an author in his field who was of interest to him in some pedagogical or scholarly way. Additionally, he had done his best to dress himself up like the Russian novelist, sporting dimestore spectacles, a long greasy beard, and a motheaten overcoat. He had grafted eye bags onto his face, too. These were departmental requirements. When I was initially interviewed for the job by the search committee, I thought it was a joke. When I later accepted the job and moved to Bliptown, I discovered it was reality. I considered reporting the instance of absurdity to the HEA (Higher Education Armada). But I couldn't afford to burn any bridges, and I had racked up unspeakable financial debt over the years. I needed a fulltime income. So I agreed to appropriate the surname of an unknown speculative fiction author whose body of work, in my view, was vastly underrated, and while I refused to get plastic surgery, I tried my best to recreate myself in his image. Fortunately I looked a lot like him. My choice wasn't well-received. But it was tolerated on the condition that my colleagues could refer to me by the nickname Blah Blah Blah.

"'Blah!" Dostoevsky shouted over the blare of the hairdryer. "Hello there!" The size of the sweat rings on his underarms indicated that he had just come back from teaching class.

"Hi Bob!" I shouted, and collapsed into my chair. The office we shared was a small, grimy dungeon. Its only light emanated from outmoded computer screens and a dim lamp that sat on Dostoevsky's desk. The paint of its stony, gunmetal grey walls flaked off in places, and there were nicks, abrasions and skid marks everywhere. In one wall was a large hole. Now and then a wild lobster crawled out and harassed us. Books didn't sit on shelves in neat, sequenced rows; they lay in dirty piles on the floor and on our desktops. There were no windows. The office was hardly the romantic portrait of plaquedemia I had envisioned when I decided to sell my soul to graduate school.

Dostoevsky sweated like an animal. It took him nearly five minutes to blowdry each armpit, and when he finished, he blowdried his eyebrows. Then he turned the machine off and began to eat a banana.

He peeled the fruit slowly, guardedly, with precision, as if it were a bomb and peeling it too fast would set it off. I tried to ignore him, observing him only out of the corners of my eyes while I prepared a lesson for my next class.

At last Dostoevsky removed the entire peel from the banana. He placed the peel in a Ziploc bag, sealed it, and deposited it in a desk drawer. After inspecting the banana for brown spots, he shoved the whole thing in his hairy mouth.

He burbled something at me. I couldn't decipher it. He burbled again. I still didn't understand. He swallowed half of his oversized mouthful and explained, "I said—bananas are my favorite fruit. Because of the potassium."

I nodded and smiled politely. "Potassium," I echoed. I didn't like my officemate. Then again, I didn't hate him. That's more or less how I felt about all human beings. "Are you teaching this afternoon?"

He swallowed more of the banana. "I'm supposed to be. I'm holding office hours instead. Nobody'll bug me that way. I haven't had a student-thing visit me on its own time in years. What about you?"

"Yeah. Advanced Neuromanticism. But I really don't feel like teaching. I'll probably send my 'gänger instead."

"Haven't you already used it once this week?"

"Yeah. But I'm just not fit to deal with my student-things' hoo-hah today. I'm hung over or something. Screw it. I'm sending my 'gänger."

Dostoevsky shrugged. He swallowed the remainder of his banana and belched.

I got out of my chair and opened the closet standing next to my desk. Inside were two androids hanging there like window-store dummies. One was a replica of Dostoevsky, the other of me. Dostoevsky enjoyed taking his android home, dressing it up like a go-go boy and sodomizing it; consequently he named it after his boyhood lover, Petunia Littlespank. I lacked the penchant for that kind of activity and named mine after the thing that plaquedemia had stolen from me: Dr. Identity. Tall and broad-shouldered with sharp, birdlike features, the android wore a Saussurian suit that changed shape, color and texture depending upon its proximity to other *en masse* fashion statements. Right now it was a neon green zoot suit like mine. Dr. Identity's eyes were florescent white and it had a scar on its forehead, the aftermath of having a wen removed by a discount street surgeon. Except for these latter two abnormalities, I was the spitting image of my 'gänger.

According to the department's faculty and student-thing handbook, assistant professors like me were allowed to use their 'gängers for only one class session per week, unlike full professors, who could use them for up to seventy-five percent of their classes. Today was the first time I would violate that stipulation. Most likely nobody would suspect the offense, and if they did, it wouldn't merit more than an invective. And I was no stranger to invectives.

I reached around Dr. Identity's head and switched it on. Sound of a fuse shorting out...Then its incandescent eyes opened, and its stiff limbs came to life.

"Hello," it said.

"Whatever," I said.

"Say hi to Petunia for me!" Dostoevsky chirped.

Dr. Identity stepped out of the closet and dusted itself off. "What day is it?"

"Thursday."

"Jesus Christ."

"Save it. Here." I handed it the half-finished lesson plan I had drawn up. "Start out with a short lecture on literary representations of contemporary cyborg bodies, using Dick and Gibson as historical reference points. Then discuss the science fiction genre's employment of Keatsian tropes and what they connote in terms of postcapitalist reality. Make sure to mention texts in which Keats appears as a cybernetic organism. After that you can do what you want. Tell jokes. Pick your ass. Just don't let anybody leave."

Dr. Identity sighed. "Okay. But for the record, I disapprove."

"Duly noted."

"People don't like you around here as it is. Especially Hemingway."

"People don't like anybody around here. And Hemingway's a jackass."

Dostoevsky removed an orange from his drawer. As he had told me many times before, it was his second favorite fruit—because of the vitamin C. He peeled the orange with the same calculated fastidiousness as the banana.

It was at this point that our resident lobster decided to make an appearance. A few days had passed since we last saw her, although we frequently heard her squeaking and growling inside of the walls. Dostoevsky and I named her Lucille after the star of the twentieth century television show *I Love Lucy*, which we both, coincidentally, had scholarly and extracurricular interest in. More than that, however, the lobster resembled Lucille Ball's hairdo in certain crouching positions. We had been trying to kill her for over six months now. But she was extremely quick, agile and easily upset. The creature crawled out of her hole and scuttled up the wall that Dostoevsky's desk was pushed up against, leaving a slimy brown residue in her wake. I carefully leaned to one side, opened a drawer, and removed a machete. Dostoevsky froze in mid-peel, chin wrinkled, eyes bulging. Dr. Identity froze, too, its eyes darting back and forth between me, my officemate and Lucille.

The lobster haphazardly scrambled across the wall, then retired to a ceiling corner. Breathing deeply, she wiped her brow with big red claws, like a boxer between rounds.

"Toss your orange over your shoulder," I whispered to Dostoevsky.

He turned his head and looked fiercely at me.

"She wants the orange," I assured him. Actually I wasn't sure what she wanted. But the orange might distract Lucille, if only for a moment. All I needed was a moment...

An agonized expression overcame Dostoevsky as if relinquishing the orange was comparable to losing a limb. He bore his rotten teeth, knitted his burly monobrow.

"Ditch that orange, sucker," I said. "Do it." I tightened my grip on the handle of the machete.

My officemate tightened his grip on the orange. "I won't do it. You can't make me do it."

Even when he was trying to speak softly, Dostoevsky had an annoyingly resonant voice. At the sound of it Lucille stopped fidgeting and cocked her head, glaring at Dostoevsky with two beady, onyx eyeballs.

I peered at Dr. Identity, pushed out my lips, and nodded.

The android lashed out. In one quick, fluid motion it slapped the orange out of my officemate's hand. The fruit splattered against the wall on the other side of the office. Dostoevsky yelped. Lucille hissed. Cocking my blade, I slipped past Dr. Identity, leapt onto Dostoevsky's desk and swung at the lobster. She dodged the blow and the machete slammed into the wall. Shards of plaster showered my face as Lucille hopped onto the ceiling and tore across it. I spun around and swung the machete up into the ceiling, missed again, made to hop off of the desk and tripped over Dostoevsky's head. Moving in fasttime, Dr. Identity strode forward. It bent over, threw out its arms, caught and positioned me on my feet.

"Thank you."

"You're welcome."

"My eye!" Dostoevsky clutched his face. The toe of my shoe had tagged him below his left eye and mauled the surgically implanted bag beneath it. "I just had this thing upgraded! Do you know how much this model costs?" He pointed helplessly at the damaged good.

Lucille emitted a high-pitched squeal from behind me. I slowly turned my head and looked over my shoulder. She lingered just above the spot where the orange had struck the wall. Her pointed head was arched up and she stared at me as if I had washed down one of her parents with a large glass of sauvignon blanc. Antennae menacingly waved back and forth.

I smirked.

Lucille shrieked.

She opened her claws and leapt at me...

It was a close call. I barely managed to duck my head out of the way. I felt one of the lobster's cold, brittle legs pass across my cheek as she sailed by...and landed on Dostoevsky's face. She didn't let go. Dr. Identity and I stared blankly at Dostoevsky as he jumped out of his chair and began to stagger around the office. Arms flailing over his head, he cursed, he cried, he smacked himself, he accused us of sabotaging him, he accused us of being jealous of his eye bags...

Eventually Lucille grew tired. She unfastened her grip and fell to the floor, taking her victim's spectacles with her. Dostoevsky's face was red, scratched and swollen. And both of his eye bags were ruined now. He stood there in a daze, blinking, gurgling...Then his eyes rolled back into his head and he fainted.

I tried to stomp on Lucille as she hastened back into her hole.

01
advanced neurorealism – 3rd person

Dr. Identity marched down the hallway carrying a briefcase in one hand and a box of homemade powdered sugar donut holes in the other. The briefcase contained three items: poorly constructed lesson plans, a hippopotamus whip, and a portable battle axe. The donut holes were for the student-things. Dr. ——— made this seemingly altruistic gesture at least twice a week to his classes, all of which met before 3 p.m. Generally speaking, student-things didn't fully awaken until about 5 p.m. The donut holes were meant to perk them up a little with a sugar high. It didn't always work, but the odds increased on the condition that, in addition to coating them in sugar, Dr. ——— also laced the donuts with ephedrine.

Between classes the hallway was a bee's nest of activity. The dogs of plaquedemia were everywhere, zipping in and out of offices with heaps of books and papers crammed beneath their armpits. Dr. Identity nodded politely at Dr. Poe, Dr. Woolf, Dr. Byron as they bumbled passed. It didn't nod at Dr. Stein. Dr. ——— had rewired his 'gänger to treat her, if only in passing, with an air of enmity and contempt. Like the modernist author she represented, "Gertie," as she wanted to be called, was an arrogant, insecure primadonna who, similar to most plaquedemics, lacked the capacity to discuss anything but herself and her scholarly work. And there's absolutely no excuse for holding a book the likes of *The Making of Amerikans* in high regard...

Dr. Identity only passed one other 'gänger on its way to class, a Charles Dickens lookalike with burning, bleached eyes like its own that had no irises, only small dark pupils. It was the one way to distinguish an android from its human counterpart. The two species hadn't always resembled each other. Just under a decade ago, androids were large, obsidian stick figures that consisted of little more than circuits, transmitters and relay switches. Once the government became a sheer corporate enterprise, funding for certain media-related technologies skyrocketed. Suddenly the exteriors of the android and the human were virtually indistinguishable.

When it arrived at the windowless steel door of the classroom, Dr. Identity rearranged its posture and methodically cracked its neck. Its pleasant smile melted into a cold, thin slit.

Its eyes blazed with white light.

The door squeaked open and the 'gänger stepped inside the classroom and slammed and locked the door behind it. Tardy student-things wouldn't be able to attend today. Present student-things wouldn't be able to leave until the period ended. Even using the toilet was forbidden: student-things were required by the university to have catheters taped to their legs during business hours for just such an eventuality.

Dr. Identity's Saussurian suit shapeshifted when confronted by the student-things' fashion statements. For females, this consisted of lace-up tube tops, Daisy Dukes and thigh high heels, despite numerous rolls of fat and patches of cottage cheese. Males, on the other hand, were caked in vast folds of denim and canvas; their heads and sneakers barely peeked out of the getups. The student-things who had sent their 'gängers to class for them dressed likewise.

Student-things were not allowed to miss class except for deaths in the family, religious holidays, and exceptionally creative lies. Mere sickness, however life-threatening, had ceased to be an acceptable excuse. A surprising number of students skipped anyway and sent 'gängers in their stead. Penalties included irreverent tongue lashings, brutal ass kickings, expulsion from the college, and public executions, depending upon the individual professor's policy.

Not all student-things could afford 'gängers, but most of them could, and the underprivileged few who couldn't took out loans to pay for them. Corndog University was a private liberal arts institution, a honeymoon suite of the Ivory Towers. Young, mediatized men and women couldn't become student-things here in the absence of sufficiently stockpiled bank vaults. More than that, though, it cost money to dress like glamtrash whores and overblown dirtbags.

Confronted by the student-things' imagistic brutality, Dr. Identity's suit began to bubble and fizz and change color. Its tie leapt out of its vest and morphed into a lightning bolt, a hissing snake, a flailing tentacle, a *sig heiling* arm and hand...The fabric of the suit rippled and undulated. Its puffed up shoulders rose, fell, gesticulated...Once the suit popped like a flashbulb, exposing the silhouette of Dr. Identity's machinic skeleton. Then it abruptly calmed down. Acclimatized to the vogue of its new environment, it was no longer the chic, sharp-looking zoot suit it used to be. Now it was a ratty, nappy-looking burlap ensemble wracked with fleas and smelling vaguely of manure. As it placed the donuts and its briefcase on a podium and prepared to address the class, Dr. Identity negotiated the new outfit by mentally dulling its sense of smell and touch.

The normative state of a student-thing's existence was a primitive state. Most of the males chased after the females. A few couples were having sex. Other males merely goosed, pet or made suggestive remarks about the objects of their desire. Or they masturbated quietly in the corners of the room while staring disinterestedly at the walls. Some females engaged in vicious catfights, biting and tearing each other's flesh off with sharply filed teeth and nails. It was a typical pre-class spectacle of sex and ultraviolence. And when Dr. Identity strode into the room, the student-things didn't skip a beat, 'gängers routinely not receiving a lick of respect.

In a loud but peaceful voice, Dr. Identity politely asked the student-things to stop antagonizing each other. It addressed a number of them by name, explaining that their conduct, if it failed to alter significantly in the next few seconds, may lead to a reduction in their overall grade for the course. Nobody listened, as Dr. Identity expected. But its program dictated that it always attempt to reconcile classroom nativism by means of the agreeably spoken word before resorting to more effective tactics.

The android gave the student-things one last chance to cease and desist. Again nobody listened. "Please St. Hellagood," it said to a young man standing in front of the podium who was nailing goose eggs into his scalp with a ball-peen hammer, "I implore you to take your seat and set an example for the rest of the class. I have donut holes. I'll give you an extra one if you do as I say." Buddy Hellagood paused for a moment and cocked his head as if contemplating obeisance. Then he swung the hammer between his legs, doubled over onto the floor, and started to dry heave.

Dr. Identity's eyes dilated until they were black. A series of switches and transmitters clicked like insects inside of its skull cavity.

Its eyes whitened. The android opened its briefcase, removed the hippopotamus whip and cracked it, screaming inarticulately at the top of its synthetic lungs. This eruption preceded a long-winded, foul-mouthed, highly articulate tirade during which Dr. Identity's whip ebbed and flowed over the heads of the student-things, occasionally digging into one of them. Soon the android began to parade around the room, raining blows on everyone. Not until it had managed to beat and strangle nearly half the student-things to within an inch of their lives did everybody settle down.

Dr. Identity loosened the whip from the neck of the student-thing in its clutches. "Right. Take a moment to pull yourselves together. Today's lecture will begin in...forty-five seconds and counting."

As it wound the hippopotamus whip around its elbow and thumb and then draped the weapon over its neck, the student-things crawled into their seats, groaning, coughing, bleeding...Some were in worse shape than others. St. Yaketyak was unconscious and had to be resuscitated with smelling salts and assisted into his seat by his peers. St. Boozealot's neck bone was sprained and had to be set in place with a popsicle stick and scotch tape. St. Blinkenod bled from multiple wounds; she licked them clean and bandaged them with torn up pieces of paper and scratch-n-sniff stickers. St. Plainjane and Bonk's 'gängers lay motionless in two crumpled piles on the floor. Dr. Identity had snapped their necks and stomped on their heads. They were legitimate kills. Ersatz professors were allowed to assassinate ersatz student-things just as non-ersatz professors were allowed to assassinate non-ersatz student-things. Given the proper circumstances, such behavior was encouraged.

The instant forty-five seconds had elapsed, Dr. Identity picked up the box of donut holes and delivered them to St. Raviolo, a pale-skinned female sitting in the front row. "Pass these out please, young miss." Like most of her counterparts, St. Raviolo possessed breast as well as love handle implants, the latter of which came into vogue last week and spread throughout the entirety of Bliptown with locustlike speed. Dr. Identity regarded her love handles idly before returning to the podium.

"Now then," the android intoned, gripping the handle of the whip with one hand and its tip with the other, "as you have no doubt discerned, Dr. ———— is incapacitated and unable to attend class today. Hence I, Dr. Identity, am here in his place...*again*. I realize that I have already substituted for Dr. ———— once this week and that doubling up, as it were, is generally considered to be atypical and, in some circles, illegal. Nonetheless I ask you all to bear with me during this troubled time."

The student-things stared at Dr. Identity like deer. A few of them had already fallen asleep in spite of their consumption of donut holes; heads tipped over their shoulders or buried in their arms, they snored soft, velvet sonatas.

Dr. Identity nodded. "Thank you for your support on this matter. Let's begin today's lesson. The topic is cyborg bodies. Would somebody be so kind as to inform me to what degree you have addressed said topic this semester?"

The student-things stared at Dr. Identity like deer. One of the sleepers slipped out of his chair, slumped onto the floor...

Dr. Identity's pupils stretched into cat's eyes. "I see. Perhaps I will assume you know nothing about cyborgs. Fine." He peered down at the lesson plans. "I shall begin with an exegesis of the term itself. *Cyborg* is a morphological blending of the terms *cybernetic* and *organism*. It was originally popularized over two centuries ago during the early 1970s and denotes any entity that is a hybrid of the human and the machine. Science fictional representations of the cyborg date back to the genre's beginnings, appearing most notably in Mary Shelley's early nineteenth century novel *Frankenstein*. If I'm not mistaken, you have already read and studied this text. Correct?"

The student-things stared at the android like deer...

Sighing, Dr. Identity decided to pretend as if the student-things were absent and it was talking to itself. It discussed the literary and theoretical history of the cyborg, carefully explicating its transition from marginalized to mainstream phenomenon. As it had been told, it made sure to cite examples from texts written by William Gibson and Philip K. Dick, among them *We Can Build You, Do Androids Dream of Electric Sheep?, The Simulacra, Neuromancer, Burning Chrome* and Gibson's posthumously published *Boohoo Mahoney and the Yesterday Kid*. He also cited more recent authors and texts like Scottrick Leete's *Ministry of Bong*, Dorian Easterbunny's *The Aluminum Occident*, and Stanley Ashenbach's *I, Ashenbach*, underscoring the great contrast between how the cyborg used to be represented and how it was represented nowadays. When it finished the lecture, Dr. Identity turned its attention to the student-things again. "Any questions about this material?"

More than half the class was sleeping now. The sugar and ephedrine had taken effect on a few student-things. Wide-eyed and fidgety, they sat bolt upright in their seats. Some gnashed their teeth. Others chewed on their cheeks. Their faces glistened with beads of sweat.

One of them raised a hand.

It was St. Von Yolk's 'gänger. Dr. Identity didn't like it. In the past it had always given it a hard time for no apparent reason—clearly St. Von Yolk had programmed it to misbehave. But it had never misbehaved to a point that Dr. Identity saw fit to exterminate it.

Dr. Identity gestured at the android. "Yes?"

The android pulled its thick, layered collar away from its mouth so that it could speak. "Fuck you," it said pointedly. Smiling, it ribbed the student-thing sitting next to it, reveling in what it perceived to be a razorsharp wit.

Student-things and their ersatz counterparts had addressed Dr. Identity far more caustically in the past. But "fuck you" would suffice for now...

In fasttime Dr. Identity removed the battle axe from its briefcase, cocked and hurled it...The blade of the axe struck its target between the eyes. The android's head exploded like a piñata. Its body toppled backwards out of its chair and crashed onto the floor. Black jelly oozed and spurted out of the gaping wound.

Petrified, the student-things who were awake stared in amazement at Dr. Identity. A few of the sleepers woke up and cursed.

"Shit," Dr. Identity parlayed.

But no. This was serious.

It rushed over to St. Von Yolk's corpse, yanked the axe out of its head, picked it up by the scruff and studied its mauled face. One white eye fell open. The pupil was a tiny, fat swastika, a symbol that no longer retained the negative connotations of Nazism since its appropriation by the loveable preteen popstar Sindie Switch.

The ball bearing that was Dr. Identity's Adam's apple rose and fell as the contact lens slipped off of the boy's eyeball and seeped onto his dead cheek.

02
luge – 1ˢᵗ person ('blah)

Petunia Littlespank was sitting on Bob Dostoevsky's lap when Dr. Identity returned to the office more than twenty minutes early. A light stench of manure lingered on its suit. I sat hunched over my desk reading a Hardy Boys novel. Petunia had applied first aid to Dostoevsky's face and made his eyebags look halfway presentable again, but he would need surgery if he wanted them to look authentic. Dostoevsky's hairy chin balanced on the android's shoulder. The android whispered tenderly in his ear and massaged his temples with its fingertips.

Dr. Identity set the briefcase on the edge of my desk. There was blood all over it.

I felt sick.

Dr. Identity said, "I think I screwed up. Big time, as they say."

"Okay. Okay." Suddenly I remembered what I had been like before entering the universe of plaquedemia: stupid, ignorant, naïve, prejudiced—the happiest asshole in the world.

"I'm to blame. There's no doubt I'm to blame. But it's not my fault. My sense of fashion is keen. But I have limitations."

I ran my tongue across my teeth. "What happened. Spit it out. That blood's the wrong color."

This got Dostoevsky and Petunia's attention. "What did you do now?" Petunia chirped.

Dr. Identity shrugged. "I murdered a student-thing. St. Von Yolk. But

31

it was an accident. I thought he was an android. He was wearing machinic contact lenses. Apparently it's a new fashion statement that surfaced yesterday and was disseminated last night via the Schizoverse. It originated in Ez, France. It was conceived of by one Bismark Pierpont, a bar tender at a poor people's casino in Monte Carlo. Pierpont derives from the Latin *De petre pont*, meaning stone bridge. Bismark is a type of jelly donut in addition to a first name. That's all I know. That was the *de facto* scoop your student-things gave me. *To be nonhuman.* Nobody told me about that kind of technodesire. I'm not programmed to identify that kind of vogue."

I closed my eyes, shook my head. Pinched the bridge of my nose.

Von Yolk. Son of Boris Von Yolk, a major player in Corndog University's Alumni Association. Over the past decade he had contributed millions. His son was a spoiled little brat who would have no doubt grown up to be a spoiled big brat like his father. But even I wouldn't have executed him. Just to be safe, I wouldn't have executed his 'gänger either.

Dostoevsky snickered. He knew how much trouble I was in.

Petunia laughed out loud.

I lost my temper...

I removed a carton of cold fried chicken from my desk and gnawed three pieces to the bone.

Dr. Identity's head drooped. "I'm sorry. My intention was not to irk you."

I patted my 'gänger on the hip. "We'll figure something out. I need a little time to think. I need a little time to think." I paused. "Did I just repeat myself?" I paused again, licking chicken grease from my lips. "Did I just repeat myself...again? Sometimes I can never remember if I repeat myself, if I repeat myself...Pardon me for a minute or two. I'll be back shortly. Don't leave this office. In the meantime, Dr. Identity, I'd appreciate it if you'd rearrange my desktop files into some sort of meaningful order. Thank you. Thank you...Thank you."

I reached behind the closet and depressed a lever. A door in the wall scraped open like a tombstone. The door scraped closed behind me as I stepped into a narrow passage, took three strides, and pivoted into another, slightly wider passage that ran parallel to my office.

A cognitive luge.

Illuminated by an industrial blacklight, the luge was a short hallway about twelve feet long just large enough to accommodate my frame. During my first month as a Corndog University employee, I had Dr. Identity hollow it out for me with a shovel and pick axe late one night. Nobody knew about it except for the occupants of my office. And nobody was allowed access to it except me. I didn't know if the luge was illegal or not. Judging from my experience with the department's illegalities so far, I assumed it was.

I retired to the luge at least once a day to pace away my anxiety. The idea came from Adolph Hitler. According to some sources, the fürher had constructed a secret room that he used solely for the "art" of pacing and meditation. Granted, his room was much larger and more luxurious than my dingy little corridor with its swinging purple light. But both served the same purposes.

Rumor had it that the speed at which Hitler paced was unparalleled, some said inhuman. In the recently discovered *Scherpilzflechte Diaries*, bodyguard Rudolf Hess claimed to have spied on Hitler through a gloryhole in the wall and clocked him with a stopwatch going over 30 mph. Apparently the faster he paced, the deeper his meditative trance. I couldn't boast that kind of speed. Even if I possessed the physical capacity to achieve 30 mph, there wasn't enough room in the luge: my elbows rubbed against the walls as I paced, and my pivoting technique was underdeveloped and awkward. Still, I could hold my own. On a good day I revved up to seven mph. But speed wasn't important right now. Right now I had to figure out what the hell to do.

Dr. Identity wasn't the first android to accidentally murder a human student-thing. Not in this department, not at this university. In fact, the practice was fairly commonplace. Unfortunately so was the punishment...

I worked up to a pace of three, maybe four mph. I may have hit five mph... Then I froze in my tracks like an exclamation point.

This is what I would do:

1. Return to my office and switch off Dr. Identity.

2. Tell Dostoevsky to do the same to Petunia and bribe him to stand by my plan with a pair of new state-of-the-art eyebag implants, plus an additional piece of plastic surgery.

3. When Dr. Hemingway comes looking for blood, explain that I was the one who killed St. Von Yolk. Like the student-thing, I had been wearing fashionable machinic contact lenses, too. Conclude with the following remark: "I have already employed Dr. Identity once this week in any event. As you and I both know, employing him again would be against the Law. I'm a tenure-track candidate. Why would I do that?"

4. When Dr. Hemingway replies, "Because it's in your nature," say, "That's a matter of opinion."

5. When Dr. Hemingway replies, "No, that's a matter of objective reality," say, "I'm sorry you feel that way."

6. When Dr. Hemingway replies, "Why would you impersonate your own 'gänger?" say, "Despite popular opinion and praxis, our profession does not preclude us from exhibiting contemporary vogue." Add the following: "At the same time, I wanted to make sure that my student-things were treating Dr. Identity with at least a modicum of respect. Hence the contact lenses functioned simultaneously as a shrewd disguise."

Here a number of eventualities may or may not arise:

A. Dr. Hemingway will rebuke me for murdering such a seminal contributor's son. He will put me in charge of establishing and maintaining a foundation dedicated to the memory of St. Von Yolk. My duties will entail sucking up to infinite grumpy old shitheads for an indefinite period of time. He will rebuke me again and stomp away in frustration.

B. Dr. Hemingway will sic Frick and Frack on me. He will excuse me from the murder of St. Von Yolk in lieu of the beating I will receive from his henchmen. He will spit on me and walk away.

C. Dr. Hemingway will ask me to produce the contact lenses that I claimed to have been wearing at the time of the murder. I will claim to have flushed them down the toilet "by accident" shortly after the "crime," which was not a crime at all, I will remind him, as it is fully within my right as an assistant professor to murder student-things at my leisure. The conversation will then manifest itself as eventuality A or B.

The plan was hardly foolproof. But it was the best I could do given my time frame. I took a sharp breath and exited the luge.

Dr. Identity was waiting for me, arms folded behind its back. Its hair and suit were disheveled. It looked guilty.

"Now what?"

Dr. Identity giggled uncomfortably...

Bathing in the blue light of his computer screen, Dostoevsky sat stiff-backed in his chair with forearms resting on thighs. His head had been twisted 180 degrees so that his chin rested between his shoulder blades. One of his eyes had popped out of its socket; it hung down his cheek like a Christmas tree ornament. A vertebra appeared to be jutting out of his neck.

Next to the computer on Dostoevsky's desk were the remains of Petunia Littlespank. The android's extremities had been ripped apart and neatly stacked atop its torso.

Fighting vertigo, I slowly turned my attention back to Dr. Identity. It looked at the ceiling. I followed suit.

Lucille. Impaled like a giant hors d'oeuvre on my machete. Twitching, moaning. I think I even detected a faint call for help.

A drop of the lobster's blood trickled down the handle of the machete and dripped onto my shoe.

I said, "Fuck."

Dr. Identity smiled a small, crooked smile. "There's more where that came from, I'm afraid." It gestured at the office door.

...Reality slipped into dreamtime. My insides seemed to leak out of my toes and I felt slightly euphoric. I floated towards the door in flashes, still shots, creeping into the future one static beat at a time. Grey roses bloomed onto my screen of vision and my diegetic universe became a silent film.

The office door opened and I jaunted into a soundless, black-and-white wax museum...

Bodies and limbs and innards littered the hallway and dangled from the ceiling. I moved through the jungle slowly at first, calculating the holocaust with the exactitude of a forensics expert. I became less attentive and more anxious the further I proceeded down the hallway. Eventually I was darting here and there at the speed of so many popping flashbulbs.

The English department bore the likeness of an exhumed graveyard. The mangled corpses of professors, student-things and their 'gängers had been strewn everywhere. The title of one of Phillip José Farmer's preneurorealist novels rattled in my head: *To Your Scattered Bodies Go*...A light, swimming fog carpeted the hallway. I could almost see it growing thicker as the internal pipes of torn open androids spit out smoke and steam...I tripped over Gertie's sluglike corpse, stumbled, and tramped on Dr. Dickens' severed head. It cracked and caved in beneath my shoe...Blood and guts oozed down the walls...A pile of ravaged student-things barred my way into the English department's main office. I climbed up the pile, lost my footing, tumbled forward and rolled into a standing position. The department secretary, Mary Kay Rumblepot, lay face down on its desk. The android was an older model. Its oily, neon brain leaked out of a hole in its onyx head.

Pieces of Frick and Frack had been stuffed into the faculty mailboxes. I recognized the monstrous jaw, the ham-fist, the antiquated brownshirt...

I flashed over to Hemingway's office door and peeked inside.

Like Mary Kay, he lay face down on his desk. Instead of a hole in his head, however, there were three plastic forks.

I walked over to him. I grabbed a fork and pulled up on it.

Professor Hemingway's beard had been ripped off of his face. In its place was a dripping chin of bone...

The smoke rose, thickened...I flashed down the hallway...

Sirens whined in the distance...

Back in my office, dreamtime reverted to realtime...I noticed a cut on Dr.

Identity's neck. Silver blood leaked from the wound. The android had retrieved Lucille from the ceiling and was turning over her corpse in its hands.

I shook my head at it in disbelief.

Dr. Identity made a frog face. "I guess I malfunctioned. But the one insurrection I committed is enough to merit the death penalty, despite its accidental nature. I figured a few more wouldn't hurt."

"You murdered the entire English department. You murdered my boss." I hesitated, overwhelmed by desperation. "How am I supposed to get tenure now?"

Dr. Identity blinked. "I don't understand the question."

The sirens were close now, and I could hear voices. If only I had time enough to revisit the luge...

"Let's go."

Dr. Identity dropped Lucille and followed me out of the office.

03
plaquedemics at large – 1st person ('blah)

Escaping the department wasn't easy. The elevator was out of commission again. I told Dr. Identity to hotwire it. The android ripped off the control panel and jammed its finger into a tangle of fiberoptics. No dice: the system had crashed.

I climbed on Dr. Identity's back, wrapped my arms around its neck and told it to head for the service stairway. The English department was on the 111th floor of the Boingboing Tower—not a chance of me descending that many floors on my own, especially in a hurry. When we emerged onto the landing, however, there was a herd of Pigs galloping towards us from two floors down. The genetically souped up pseudonyms-made-flesh flaunted German war helmets, oversized Fisher Price mirrorshades and martial arts weaponry. Surrogates of the police, they would tear us to shreds with ease. I got off Dr. Identity's back, pulled it back into the department, slammed and bolted the door.

The smoke in the hallway had swelled to our waists. We hurried back to my office, stumbling over corpses and body parts, and retrieved my jetpack. I looked around for Dostoevsky's piece. No sign of it. He must have taken a worm to work today.

I strapped the jetpack onto Dr. Identity. We darted back into the hallway just as the Pigs burst through the door. They chased us to the end of the hallway, hurling throwing stars, tessens, kamas, sais and Kozuka blades at our backs.

We dove through a tall bay window and vanished in an explosion of glass shards.

We freefell a half mile before Dr. Identity managed to activate the jetpack. Its obsolete, refurbished engine once belonged to a lawnmower and required a pull-string to start it. An apocalyptic scream lit a fire in my throat. Dr. Identity sported a calm, almost bored expression as he turned end over end and fiddled with the jetpack.

The contraption finally came to life. My 'gänger grabbed me by the armpits. We leveled out and I stopped screaming.

We ascended into traffic.

"Where to?" shouted Dr. Identity.

I tried to respond, but my voice was gone.

I pointed at the heart of the city.

Bliptown was an immense junkyard of architectures and geometries, a hulking assemblage of suburbs and strip malls that had been crammed together and stacked on top of each other. But a certain orderliness prevailed despite the swarms of construction beams that always-already swung across the city's ever expanding periphery. Viewed from high enough in the air, Bliptown seemed to be breathing, inhaling and exhaling like a live thing. Its neoindustrial exterior mainly consisted of flickering neon logos, insignias, business monikers and vidbuildings showcasing the latest fashion statements, newsflashes, commercials and porno fetishes.

Flyways coursed across the skin of the city like varicose veins. Glinting, fire-breathing machinery flowed and surged in every direction. Dr. Identity and I weaved through the traffic, dodging as many construction beams as aircrafts, and slipped into an indiscrete alaristrian lane. There was no speed limit, but most of the alaristrians weren't going more than 40 mph except for a few teenagers who darted to and fro like gnats.

We couldn't go back to my cubapt. The Pigs would be waiting for us and no doubt destroying or pocketing whatever they could get their hooves on. They had probably given my wife-thing a going over by now. If she was still alive, divorce papers were imminent. I needed to get used to loss. In the wake of Dr. Identity's act of ultraviolence, my life would never be the same again.

The Law in Bliptown was an automated speed demon. A few seconds after we dove out of the English department, an *en masse* APB was surely put out on us. Probably we would sail past a vidbuilding in the next minute or two showcasing our colossal wanted-dead-or-alive images.

To make matters worse, there was the legality of vigilantism to consider. In addition to the surrogates of the Law, Dr. Identity and I could also expect the families of the student-things, professors and 'gängers it killed to hunt us down—with the full support of Bliptown's governing powers. If we wanted to survive, we needed more weapons than Dr. Identity's hands and feet.

And we had no credit. No means of using credit anyway. The moment I spent a penny, the Law would have us.

Hunger besieged me.

High anxiety always had that effect. The more I worried, the more I ate— and needed to eat. Deathlike feelings accompanied boiling points. And they weren't infrequent. A speedy metabolism helped me maintain a slender figure. Right now I felt like challenging the power of that metabolism. I reached up and tugged on Dr. Identity's suit.

Dr. Identity glanced down at me. "What!"

"Sandwich," I squeaked.

"What!"

I arched back my head so the android could see my mouth. "*Sand-wich.*"

Dr. Identity frowned. "You know I can't read lips! What's the matter with you!"

I pointed at my stomach. I punched myself in the face.

"Oh." Dr. Identity's pupils splashed against its eyeballs like mosquitoes on a windshield as it calculated what to do...

It exited the flyway and ascended to the rooftop of a nearby vidbuilding with a shopshack. It dropped me onto my feet. I tripped and fell into an ungainly somersault. Dr. Identity picked me up, dusted me off, and slapped me.

"What was that for?"

"Pain helps sometimes."

Dr. Identity

The rooftop's aesthetic was minimalist-medieval. A few stone tables and chairs near the edges. Tall, hollow suits of armor here and there. The shopshack was a rickety wooden structure that wore its merchandise on the outside. Inside crouched vendors in buzzard suits.

Not much of a crowd on the rooftop. A handful of cow-pigeons casually devoured whatever pieces of trash they could get their beaks on. Some alaristrians drank coffee, shined mirrorgoggles, cleaned their business suits with oversized lint brushes. Most were 'gängers, which wasn't atypical in the public sector: corporate subjects surrogated themselves with much more frequency than plaquedemics.

A small group of 'gängers had gathered around an allotriophagic mime. Every minute or two, the mime spontaneously regurgitated a sequence of random, nonedible objects, took a garish bow, and held his bowler hat out for spare change. Now he disgorged what appeared to be a collection of small mechanical clocks. The timepieces dribbled out of his mouth and formed a pile between his feet. The audience observed the spectacle with a cool disconnectedness, idly checking their watches to see if they were synchronous with the mime's vomit.

The canvas of sky overhead was a dull orange color. Sharp, thin clouds peeled across it in neat droves as if drawn there with an Etch-A-Sketch.

A shelf of prepackaged sandwiches caught my attention.

"I'm hungry," I wheezed

"I know," Dr. Identity said.

I licked my lips. "Garlic bologna."

Dr. Identity strode to the shopshack. I told it to stop. "Wait. Wait. We can't pay for anything."

It kept going. I let it.

We were in trouble when we landed on the rooftop. Shortly after we left the rooftop, we were among the Papanazi's ten most wanted snapshots.

Dr. Identity began fumbling through a row of sandwiches.

A claw reached out of the shopshack and grabbed the android by the wrist.

Dr. Identity looked at the claw quizzically, then looked up. Two yellow eyes peered out of the shadows.

"Buy or fly," said a snakelike voice.

Dr. Identity tried to shake its hand free of the vendor's grip. "Get your mitt off of me."

"Get your mitt off of my sandwiches."

The android's eyes pulsed. Within reach was a copper vase that contained a bouquet of Baasendorfer samurai swords. The vase sat atop a large antique television set. A syndicated episode of the science fictionalized version of *Leave It to Beaver* was on. I had seen the episode before. There was no plot or dialogue, only a scikungfi Battle Royal that took place between June Cleaver and Eddie Haskell in the living room. For a moment Dr. Identity seemed to be hypnotized by the show.

Then its head stiffened, its lips convulsed.

Moving in fasttime, it pulled a sword out of the vase and sliced off the vendor's claw. The vendor shrieked. Dr. Identity reached into the shopshack and yanked it out by the neck. Feathers snowed off of its buzzard suit...

Dr. Identity tossed the vendor into the air and sliced it in half.

The vendor's torso landed flat on its back. It panted, squirmed, gesticulated as its innards poured out like baked beans.

The vendor's waist and legs pinwheeled out of control and struck a flâneur. He was a refined-looking gentleman wearing a top hat, mirrormonocle and razorcoat with tails. Somehow the legs wrapped around his chest and neck, then a foot kicked him in the head, knocking him cold.

Dr. Identity made quick work of him.

The severed head of the flâneur bounced past me like a discarded basketball, its mirrormonocle firmly in place.

Not until the head bounced off the roof did I process the murders. They both transpired in under ten seconds.

"Maniac!" I rasped. Somebody screamed.

Dr. Identity lobbed me a sandwich. "Relax. Eat that before you really freak out. It's haggis and cheese. Closest thing I could find to garlic bologna. Excuse me for a moment."

"No." The sandwich hit me in the chest and fell on my feet.

Full of purpose and resolve, Dr. Identity brandished the samurai sword, swung it around its body with ninjalike dexterity, turned and leapt into the shopshack. The structure quaked and splintered. It collapsed when my 'gänger exited through a chimney pipe, somersaulting across the orange sky as if shot out of a cannon.

Dr. Identity landed squarely on its feet and didn't falter. In addition to the vendors, it massacred everyone on the rooftop, including the allotriophagic mime. The mime tried to strike back, regurgitating and spitting hatchets at its attacker. But he was far too slow and had poor aim.

When it was over, the android flung the sword aside and strolled over to me. My face was a blank slate. The haggis sandwich lay at my feet. Dr. Identity picked it up and handed it to me. "I thought you were hungry? Eat this. Take it."

I wasn't hungry anymore. Anxiety gave way to rage. I slapped the sandwich out of its hand. "Are you kidding me?"

"Kidding?" Dr. Identity said. "There's nothing funny about this scenario."

"Scenario?"

Dr. Identity smirked. "Think of me as your Id, 'Blah. You can play Ego. How does that sound?"

I regarded my 'gänger hatefully. "Don't call me 'Blah. Nobody can call me that anymore."

"Pardon me. At any rate, as I already made clear, our actions no longer matter."

"*Our* actions?"

"You know what I mean. Who cares if I imbibe in a little serial killing at this point? We're both going to die. It's just a matter of time. Are you all right? Don't tell me you're experiencing some kind of moral dilemma. Why would a solipsistic misanthrope like you care about the lives of other organisms?"

Dr. Identity had never spoken to me with such frankness and hostility. Clearly the trauma of the initial, accidental killing of St. Von Yolk had driven it insane.

"I...I..."

Dr. Identity frowned. "What is it?" It glanced over its shoulder.

Across the street from the vidbuilding beneath us was the Quicksilver Spire. Its mirrored exterior contained the colossal, distorted images of Dr. Identity and me. The footage had been shot by Dostoevsky one afternoon in our office. Both of us stared listlessly into the minicam...

I ran to the edge of the rooftop. Beneath our images in giant lettering was an announcement:

PLAQUEDEMICS AT LARGE!!!

Sirens dopplered towards us through the caterwaul of traffic in the flyways.

I glared at Dr. Identity. "Come on."

We ditched my prehistoric jetpack and stole two new ones. Mine was an AK-Zingblinger. Other than being drenched in blood, it was in tiptop shape. I removed it from a soaking torso and strapped it on.

Dr. Identity was in the air first, gesturing for me to hurry up.

I retrieved the haggis and cheese sandwich before obliging him.

04
incognito – first person (identity)

Dr. ——— suggested that we disguise ourselves. I agreed. We descended into the mechanical depths of Bliptown. The technetronic strata of strip malls reminded me of a futuristic version of Dante's *Inferno*. I always wished I could read *Inferno* in the original Italian. For whatever reason Dr. ——— refused to download the language into my lexicon.

We landed in an alleyway outside of a ghost mall.

Landings weren't Dr. ———'s forte. He came down and tripped over a Beesuppie (Brett Easton Ellis-Style Urban Professional) who had been taking a nap next to a dumpster. The Beesuppie was scratched and stained. He wore a limited edition Calloway Italian-knit golf shirt and Mondale Duego khaki pants and gray leather armadillo-skinned boat shoes. He bleated when Dr. ——— ran into him. He stumbled to his feet and groggily began to complain about his job and his wife and the taste of his breakfast.

I made a fist and struck the Beesuppie on top of the head. He crumbled. I removed his clothes and threw him into the dumpster.

"Here." I tossed Dr. ——— the clothes.

I walked to the far side of the alleyway where a gang of other Beesuppies was taking a collective nap. I sized them up. I selected one. I hit him and removed his clothes: short-sleeve Gatsby mercerized shirt and white no-wrinkle Van Rotten dress pants with pink pinstripes and forgettable leather sandals.

Taking off my Saussurian suit felt good. I was tired of being preyed upon by

47

other people's fashion statements. The suit struggled in my grasp as I ushered it over to the dumpster and deposited it inside. It jumped out and tried to put itself back on me. I punched and kicked it and returned it to the dumpster. I placed the body of a Beesuppie atop the dumpster's lid to insure the suit wouldn't escape again.

I stood naked and watched Dr. —— wriggle into the golf shirt and khakis and put on the boat shoes.

"The shoes are too tight," he complained. "And my pants are wrinkled. And I hate the color of this shirt."

"They're fine. You look fine. Relax."

"I don't want to relax." He adjusted and readjusted his shirt collar and waistband. "I need a belt." He cursed loudly. "My voice hurts." He cursed softly. "I need a doctor. I'm in agony."

"Jesus. Hold on." I put on the clothes...

He tried to shoo me away when I reached out for his neck. I told him to grow up. He told me to eat shit. I asked him why he was acting like a child. He said I had no business comparing him to a child as I was a machine and a monster and lacked the ability to conceive of human behavior in its primitive form not to mention its adult form. I told him not to be unfriendly. He told me that unfriendliness begets unfriendliness.

I clutched his windpipe.

He barked and gasped and ordered me to unhand him. I waited until my fingertips had secreted enough fluid...

"You son of a bitch," Dr. —— said. He rubbed his neck. "Now it feels worse."

"No it doesn't. Of course it doesn't."

A nearby Beesuppie pushed himself to his feet and drowsily began practicing his golf swing. He had on a Gila monster-skinned Crocodile Dundee hat and a buttondown flywing shirt and Damascus driving gloves and an Isle of Skye kilt and bleached white kneehigh socks. He didn't have on shoes. Dr. —— and I stared at him. He swung too hard. He got tangled up in his own limbs. He fell back down.

Dr. ——— said, "Corndog University wasn't so horrible. The English department wasn't so horrible. I'm the horrible one. I'm the asshole. If people don't agree with me, if they don't think the way I do and place value on the things I do, if they aren't as good-looking as me—I condemn them. I sentence them to Worthlessness. Without due process." He started to pace back and forth and quickly achieved an impressive speed for a human. "That's why I don't have any friends. That's why you're my only friend. My 'gänger. My *Id*. And what does my goddamn Id do? Fucking kills the whole world."

"Isn't that what Ids are supposed to do?"

He ignored me. "I'm going to miss that place. I really am. Dostoevsky—he wasn't a bad man. A bit eccentric, but who isn't? I liked Petunia, too, when they weren't all over each other. We once had an excellent conversation about the short stories of Nikolai Gogol, and that android could make a mean cup of Kool-Aid. I often catch myself thinking about its Kool-Aid. I was just thinking about it a moment ago, in fact. I even liked Lucille. I liked her a little anyway. If nothing else she spruced up the social climate of the office. And Hemingway had his admirable qualities. He once allowed me to take an extra fork without saying a thing about it out of the goodness of his heart. I didn't care much for the other faculty members with the exception of Dr. Shelley, but that's just because she had nice tits and well-defined calves. Her face was another matter. The point is, I didn't like my colleagues, but they didn't bug me. They let me be for the most part. What more can a bastard like me ask from my fellow assholes? Hell, even my student-things had redeeming qualities. Some of them anyway. At least I didn't want to kill myself every single time I taught a class. Only fifty percent of the time. Sixty percent at most. Things were adequate enough in that English department. They weren't unbearable. Things are a lot worse in other departments, at other universities. A lot worse. I know this guy who teaches at Hogwash College. 'Gängers are illegal there! I couldn't imagine teaching all of my classes by myself. I can't believe this mess. I can't believe *you*. You've ruined my life. You've ruined everything I've worked for. Do you know how much free time I had on my hands? It really wasn't necessary for me to work more than ten hours a week, including teaching, the most unfortunate drawback of my profession. The rest of the time I could just dick around and read and write to my heart's content. I spent eight years of my life in graduate school for nothing because of your goddamn antics. Are you proud of yourself you goddamn lunatic?" He stopped pacing and faced me.

I was silent.

Dr. ———— unleashed a long-winded pyrotechnic surge of obscenities. It was an admirable surge and exceptionally lyrical and my original invented several alluring neologisms. The persistent spray of spittle on my face was disagreeable. But I waited patiently for him to tire out.

"Are you finished?"

Sweat glistened on Dr. ————'s overlip and brow. He caught his breath and said, "Yes. For now at least. But you will admit you've been acting like a psychopath. You *are* a psychopath. Something's wrong with your program. You need help. *We* need help."

"We need to be alert," I insisted. "And nothing is wrong with my program. How many times do I have to tell you? My program is a crystalline manifestation of..."

My ears sharpened into antennae as my radar picked up the newsflash. It emanated from an old Philco 84B Classic Cathedral radio somewhere inside the ghost mall. The cold black pupils engulfed the warm whites of my eyes. For a moment I went blind.

Dr. ———— knew the score. He just couldn't hear it. "What's the matter? What're you receiving?"

"Quiet."

My vision slowly faded back in as the whites recolonized the landscape of my eyeballs.

"Oops." My ears returned to their normal state.

"Oops? Oops what? What is it? Oops what?"

I flexed the muscles in my abdomen. "It looks like I've made another little booboo. Yes indeed. Apparently I've managed to murder Voss Winkenweirder. According to the Papanazi, I took his life during my most recent killing spree. Of course he was incognito and I had no way of knowing who he was. Do you recall the flâneur I chopped in half? A fine disguise. He must have been wearing a mask, too. Oh well. Even if I had known it was him, I probably would have killed him anyway. Without question I would have killed him. At any rate, the whole world is after us. Dead or alive, we're worth more than Winkenweirder's paycheck for his last three films combined."

Dr. ———— cleared his throat. "You killed...a movie star?"

"Apparently so. How about that? Not many humans can say they've killed a movie star, especially one of such notoriety. Not bad for a simulacrum."

Once again Dr. ———— resorted to verbal pyrotechnics.

Sometimes it was legal to kill movie stars. Particularly if they appeared in a bad film or their acting lacked sufficient realspace credibility. The legality was recently established to encourage filmmakers and their entourages to produce quality artwork as opposed to the trash the last two centuries had seen them put out. Not so with Voss Winkenweirder. The actor invariably starred in superb films and his performances were always watertight. The unsubstantiated murder of such a hypercelebrity would not only guarantee our deaths. It would guarantee torture and very likely public disembowelment. Dr. ———— had good reason to be upset. Nonetheless I put an end to his hysterics with a firm backhand across the face that sent him spinning. I caught him and apologized. He stared at me dumbly. I told him I didn't strike him to shut him up. I did it to safeguard his voice box. Then I explained how I actually enjoyed the aesthetic beauty of his foul-mouthed diatribes. They demonstrated an industrious use of the imagination.

"Thank you, Dr. Identity," whispered Dr. ————.

I shrugged. "That's what friends are for."

05

littleoldladyville, part 1 – 1ˢᵗ person ('blah)

It was no use trying to escape Bliptown. The whole world knew about us now. No doubt commodity-paraphernalia created in our image was already in production. As early as tomorrow morning I expected to find Dr. ——— and Dr. Identity action figures in store windows. Our avatars were probably already for sale in the Schizoverse. Variations of our names would soon be affixed to jetpacks, hairdos, fast food. Book sales of the author I surrogated were probably on the verge of skyrocketing. No matter where we went, we would be hunted by countless human and machinic extensions of the Law. Every city on Earth and Mars was immediately accessible via the Schizoverse anyway. Bliptown seemed as good a place as any to suffer and die.

We could flee to the artificial rainforests, which had been constructed on the few remaining land masses between the cities. But that was tantamount to suicide. The last remaining agents of photosynthesis, the rainforests were full of mechanical dinosaurs, abominable snowmen, Frankenstein monsters, King Kongs and other artificial creatures disseminated by the government in order to discourage people from settling outside urban interzones. Dr. Identity and I wouldn't last more than an hour in the wilderness. We were better off fending for ourselves against our fellow anthropomorphous assholes.

Initially the murder of Voss Winkenweirder terrified me. But I got over it. I no longer cared about what happened to us, and the fear of death dwindled to a dull, barely recognizable pulse somewhere in the basement of my emotional townhouse. At that moment I didn't care about anything. I would very likely be dead within the next twenty-four hours. It didn't matter. I had committed no actual crime myself. But Dr. Identity's crimes were as good as my own. That's a risk of purchasing and employing a 'gänger: the user is entirely responsible for his commodity's actions. Before today I had been unwilling to take that responsibility. Now I was unconditionally willing.

This psychological numbness lasted for about thirty seconds. Then it disappeared, instantly, as if ripped out of me.

I screamed.

Dr. Identity picked me up and shook me. It set me back down.

I vomited. I cursed it for shaking me so hard.

"Your conduct, your discourse, and the flows of your desires belong to a child," said the android. "I would prefer it if you acted like an adult from now on. At least play an adult."

I blinked.

The Beesuppie Dr. Identity had thrown in the garbage crawled out. He slipped as he tried to throw his leg over the edge of the dumpster and landed on his face. His neck cracked. An uncannily bright red pool of blood oozed out of his mouth, nostrils and eyes.

Dr. Identity admired the pool. "Hammer blood," it said. "I wish my veins pumped that piece of trendiness." It bent over and inspected the blood with wide-eyed curiosity. "To inject vogue into the body—the ultimate fashion statement."

The accidental death of the Beesuppie shocked me back into coherence.

"We have to go," I said.

"Go where?"

"Littleoldladyville."

Dr. Identity glared at me. "Why would we do a thing like that?"

"Because I say so. Get your jetpack on."

Littleoldladyville was an ADW (Allpurpose Department Warehouse), which sold virtually every product imaginable. Imaginations themselves were available in a range of brands, styles and creative angles of incidence. While cheap, an imagination cost arms and legs to download. Most shoppers couldn't afford it. And those that could afford it—the student-things that attended Corndog University, for instance—were uninterested in them. They gravitated more towards products like 'gängers, Schizoverse avatars, innovative slang terms (decreed commodities by the Law only last Spring), prosthetic genitals, disco and break dance moves, alternate voices, and other indicators of "personality."

Littleoldladyville recently assimilated its last remaining competitors, rendering it the only extant ADW in the Amerikanized world. Every major city harbored five or six of them, and their great bulk constituted roughly thirty percent of each city's superstructure. It was easy to get lost inside. I once got so lost it took me almost three days to get out. Precisely the idea. The elusive, labyrinthine structure of the ADW prohibited many shoppers from finding their way out when they wanted to. In order to maintain a sufficiently breakneck flow of consumerism under such conditions, a law was imposed: *No customer will exist for more than thirty minutes without buying at least $100 worth of products under the penalty of death.*

Products could only be bought by means of retinal scans. Cashiers had gone extinct. All a shopper needed to do was run a product's barcode across its eyes. At birth everybody's vision was registered with the government so that they could buy things simply by looking at them. If shoppers failed to make a purchase inside of thirty minutes, a mechanical Bug-Eyed Monster attacked and swiftly tore them to pieces. Littleoldladyville had impeccable surveillance technology. On the occasion of my going astray, I forgot to buy something within the designated time frame, and just moments after a half hour elapsed, I heard the monster scuttling towards me from a nearby aisle. Luckily I made a purchase before it made an appearance. Although horrifying, the BEM was a nice touch from a literary perspective—yet another instance of reality imitating science fiction. In the end my three day misadventure skidrowed me. But I was already skidrowed. Everybody was always-already skidrowed.

The name *Littleoldladyville* had been devised by its founder, Hilda

Grumpstead. Coincidentally she was a little old lady at the time of the name's conception. A profound love as a child for her grandmother Babetta, a shopping queen who had won awards for her many consumer-capitalist accomplishments, had invoked a lifelong fantasy of a superstore full of grandmotherlike beings who might consume products to their heart's content. Not until Hilda was a grandmotherlike being herself did she amass enough capital and technopolitical clout to bring her pipe dream to life. By then Babetta was long dead, although she had recreated an android in her image. She had recreated thousands of them. And whereas Hilda died last century and Littleoldladyville was hardly the utopian superstore she originally envisioned, the machinic versions of little old Babetta continued to populate the store—as managers, stock girls, aisle guards, mannequins, consumer spies, in-house plastic surgeons, and shoppers themselves. This demographic was complimented by the majority of the ADW's shopping community, which predominantly included little old ladies and their 'gängers. Some came there to die. Others refused to let elderliness get their goats; for them, Littleoldladyville was an opportunity to prove that they still possessed youthful (or at least middle-aged) spunk. Others were senile and psychotic.

In addition to weapons and food, Littleoldladyville offered us new disguises. Our current disguises were necessary but unacceptable. We lacked facial hair and accoutrements, and the clothes were old, faded and unfashionable. Dr. Identity wouldn't tolerate it for long. I could barely tolerate it.

Littleoldladyville also featured scores of surgery booths where we could have our faces reconstructed by a skilled Babetta. Facelifts were something to consider, but ultimately we didn't need them. If we managed to evade the Law for long enough, eventually the thrill of the hunt would wear off and the government would set its DNA hounds on our tails. No matter where we fled, we would be sniffed out. First we had to concentrate on camouflaging ourselves with *en vogue* body armor and stocking up on our present arsenal of weapons, which now consisted solely of Dr. Identity's appendages. The android was clearly an able-bodied killer. But going into Littleoldladyville amounted to going to war. And we lacked both the means and the intention to pay for our share of the battle.

We activated our jetpacks and ascended into the dark, contorted spiral of strip malls above us. Dr. Identity took the lead. I followed him through a web of flyways, shielding my face with my collar, dodging traffic, and trying not to focus on the torrent of images that accosted us at every turn. Bliptown was alive with our electronic headshots and Winkenweirder film clips, and Papanazis were ubiquitous, digitizing everything and everyone. Most were easily distinguishable. Jetpackers wore large Grim Reaper exoskeletons and robes, and the Papanazi standard issue vehicle was a souped-up Third Reich warplane, the Heinkel He-162 Volksjaeger. I had expected this kind of mayhem, but being in the middle of it terrified me. I pulled next to Dr. Identity and told him to speed up.

Babettas guarded either side of the palatial, Romanesque entrance of Littleoldladyville. They were about five feet tall, including the beehive hairdos, and signified late octogenarians. The original Babetta had been addicted to tanning booths and a dull orange color tinted their leathery skin. Their faces were sharp and birdlike. A hairy mole was artfully positioned on their chins, and coke bottle spectacles sat on their noses. The spectacles magnified their white, irisless eyes to an estranging degree. Hairy shawls covered their hunchbacks. Their pencil-thin legs were sheathed in netted stockings with fashionable tears in them. From afar, they looked like neckless, over-the-hill ostriches. They didn't look much different close up.

Shoppers marched in and out of the entrance in a fluid, orderly swarm. Like the Babettas, most of them were short, frail-looking, and blue-haired. Dr. Identity and I stuck out like spraypainted sequoias as we slipped into the swarm and made for the door.

I nodded politely at the Babettas as we passed. They didn't nod back. They stared at me with their giant eyes. One of them growled.

We entered the store and checked our jetpacks with another Babetta. It was illegal to bring anything into Littleoldladyville except the clothes on our backs, items that were themselves suspect, especially since most fashion statements entailed outrageously baggy outfits, the perfect hideaway for stolen merchandise. In effect, the ADW's current board of directors was involved in litigation to have clothes banned from it. Soon the only permissible style of clothing on store grounds would be a birthday suit.

The Babetta flicked us a number and shuffled into a long, narrow hanger, dragging our jetpacks behind it like two dead animals. We would of course never see them again. This wasn't a problem. If we lived, Littleoldladyville carried a vast array of jetpacks. We would simply add them to our list of needful things.

"I'm hungry," I whispered out of the corner of my mouth. The stench of hot cabbage in the air grew stronger and thinned out as clusters of little old ladies toddled past us.

Dr. Identity narrowed its eyes at me. "Why are you whispering?"

I gnawed on my lip. "I don't know," I said in a normal voice. "Anyway, I'm hungry. But we need weapons first."

"I know what we need. I know you're hungry. You don't have to keep telling me. Over and over you tell me." The android surveyed the insane parade of aisles that stretched over and ahead of us like a galactic cornfield. "We need an entropy projector. And organic weaponry. Biological claws, tentacle wads, piranha balls, maybe a few monsters-in-a-can. We'll want vibronic munitions. A glaive for me and a tetronix for you. Cutting edges are essential. Fusion stilettos, razor fans, razor tentacles, toxic flechettes, force projector shurikens. I'd like a hypersharp Vorpal sword. And a monofilament whip. And a razorwire yo-yo. We shouldn't forget about guns. I prefer blades, but one likes to be well-rounded. We would do well to amass everything from idiot guns to biologic, electric, psychic, metaphysical, phenomenological and linguistic firearms—the latter three for kicks, of course. I've always wanted to pump someone full of French turns-of-phrase with a *raison d'être* MK-7. I've always wanted to turn someone's reality inside-out with a stream of excited quarks fired from a lepton pistol. We don't have time for these kinds of fun and games. But one likes to keep up an air of theatrics."

My 'gänger spoke in a detached monotone. I didn't know if it was kidding or serious. Either way, it was unwell. I wondered when psychosis would fully set in and short-circuit its nervous system.

"I've let you teach too many science fiction classes," I said.

Dr. Identity's pupils mutated into large asterisks. "It's possible. More likely, however, I'm just a product of the future. And the future's been extinct for a long time."

06
achtung 66.799 & co. – 3rd person

Achtung 66.799 came up with the idea of a stainless steel cuckoo clock while doing secretarial work for Dodo, Meese & Bolshevik, a company that produced the number six for several successful brands of holographic, digital and corporeal clock faces. At the time he was getting reprimanded by the secretary-in-chief for fooling around in the Schizoverse during working hours. The secretary-in-chief was being surrogated by her 'gänger. Its breath smelled like sulfur. Achtung 66.799 stared over its shoulder at the antiquated Weiner wood cuckoo clock hanging on the wall as the android accused him of laziness, lack of enthusiasm, a mild case of anthropomorphism, and "inexorable loutishness." The clock struck nine, a door irised open, and a mechanical bird tentatively poked out its head. It was Tuesday and the clock's real bird, a clone of a crimson-breasted shrike, had the day off. Although new and tentative about telling the time, the surrogate finally produced an irresolute squawk.

The surrogate was made of stainless steel. Achtung 66.799 liked the way it gleamed in the light of the office. The guise worked for the bird. Why not for a whole clock?

"Hey!" shouted the secretary-in-chief's 'gänger. "Pay attention to me when I'm tearing you a new asshole!"

Achtung 66.799 nailed the android with a right hook. The punch broke two of his knuckles. He screamed out his resignation and puttered to the nearest surgery stand on the broken wings of a blue-collar jetpack.

61

As a street surgeon rebuilt his knuckles, he mulled over the particulars of his would-be new invention, wondering where he might get the capital to produce it. There were also the formalities of cuckoo clock copyrights and a patent to consider. He didn't know shit about those things. Nor did he know much about clocks in general. He barely knew how to tell time.

Achtung 66.799 realized that quitting his job may not have been the wisest course of action. He was too proud to beg for it back. But it didn't matter. Within minutes of his departure surely a fresh assistant secretary replaced him. He would have to get another job. Fast. He only had enough savings to last him six, seven hours at most...

The next morning he secured a position as a lawn jockey. Had he kept track, he would have discovered that this was the 183rd position he had secured in his young adult life.

The two and a half square footage of yard he had to pose on was rather large considering its location in a densely populated neighborhood and rooftop. He had plenty of room to stretch on the occasion that nobody looked in his direction and caught him not being perfectly frozen and sculpturelike.

His outfit consisted of a glazed white terracotta helmet, a skintight red riding coat, beige polyester pants that flared out at the thighs, and shiny black kneehigh boots. Now and then the owner of the lawn, Mr. Archibald Grapesmuggler, asked him to dress up in blackface.

Things went smoothly for a few days. He came to work on time every morning, posed, took a break for lunch, posed, and left at dusk. Then he let his guard down. He came to work with a hangover. A bad one. He could barely keep his eyes open. And his arm hurt: the strain of holding up a kerosene lamp seemed insufferable. Thinking nobody was watching, he lowered the lamp and sat down on the grass for a minute to rest. Seconds later he was curled up in a fetal position, snoring and drooling.

He didn't know that his employer had been spying on him from a gopher hole in the lawn.

Mr. Grapesmuggler pushed his head through the hole and crawled out like a zombie from the grave. Achtung 66.799 woke up, tendered his resignation, and ran away...

He came back a few minutes later and said he was sorry. Mr. Grapesmuggler accepted the apology and handed him a handkerchief. "You're drooling."

An idea came to him. It wasn't like the others. This one was sound, realizable—an anti-drool serum. One specifically designed to turn off (or at least tone down) salivary ducts during sleep. His friend Dale Begonia dabbled in street chemistry. The two of them could invent such a commodity extraordinaire if they put their minds together. And once it appeared on the market, the split would be 70/30 in favor of Achtung 66.799. He would market the product, after all, and marketing was more valuable than scientific innovation and practice. The value of science was in fact only as good as the marketability of the merchandise produced by science. He rethought the split and decided on 80/20. He rethought three more times and finally settled on 86/14. Then he kneed Mr. Grapesmuggler in the nuts and tendered his resignation a second time...

The plan failed. Dale Begonia turned out to be more of a hack than he thought; apparently his skills as a chemist didn't go much further than a rudimentary knowledge of the periodic table, an ability to define the term *isotope*, and holding test tubes full of Sea Monkeys over Bunsen burners until they boiled and exploded. Achtung 66.799 had also forgotten about the patent again. The blow to his optimism was devastating. He went on a drinking binge that lasted a half hour before the time came to sober up and find (and lose) another job.

Over the next year, he found (and lost) work as a stapler slammer, an underapprentice to a magician, an assistant palm reader, an assistant moth wrangler, an assistant to an assistant eyebrow plucker, a window shade, a pied piper, and a turtleneck dickey model, among others. For a while he was even subcontracted by a 'gänger to surrogate the human high school teacher that the 'gänger was supposed to be surrogating.

All the jobs ended the same way: Achtung 66.799's imagination took advantage of his better judgment.

"I have so many ideas," he told Dale one night as they sat in his 1/3-bedroom cubapt on either side of a Bunsen burner drinking glasses of Rippentrop's Foggy Foggy Dew. "I don't know what to do with myself. The world can't keep up with me."

"You also don't have a graduate degree," Dale noted. "A man can't do anything without a graduate degree these days. If you misbehave, they kill you in some cities without one, or at least feed you to a rainforest. Happened to a friend of mine in Synthesizer City. Eddie Horkheimer was his name. Papanazi said the Law caught him philosophizing in public without a Ph.D. They catapulted him over the city walls and a fucking three-headed dinosaur mutilated and devoured him before he even hit the ground. Papanazi caught the whole thing. No shit. I think I might even have a clip of it lying around here somewhere." He began to dig through the piles of debris that littered his cubapt.

Achtung 66.799 took a swig of Foggy Foggy Dew. The drink billowed into his mouth. "I once knew a guy named Eddie who shaved the hair off of his body and it grew back the wrong way. The hair grew backwards, I mean, inside of his body. Except for his face and scalp. I remember his chest and back was so bushy he looked like a porcupine or something. It was the first time he'd shaved his whole body. Maybe the hairs did it out of revenge. They felt betrayed and weren't expecting to be offed. Maybe he had some kind of subcutaneous condition. Whatever the reason, eventually the little bastards got so long they strangled and suffocated all of his muscles and internal organs. Once he realized what was going on, he tried to have them surgically removed, but they were too long and there were too many of them. Eddie's autopsy showed that before he died he was really just a scarecrow, stuffed from neck to ankle in wet black hay. Talk about ingrown hairs."

Dale looked at him. "Is that true?"

"Does it matter?" Achtung 66.799 hit his bottle until it was empty. "The point is I don't want to end up like a goddamn scarecrow."

"What's a scarecrow got to do with your situation?"

Achtung 66.799 thought about the question. "I don't know what it has to do with me. It's just that getting killed by your hair is lousy. That's all. And I feel lousy. I always feel lousy."

"Maybe you need a new hobby." Dale returned to his search for the clip of Eddie Horkheimer's execution.

"I don't need a new hobby. I need a lobotomy. I'm sick of thinking about things. All day long, all I do is think about things. My brain's like a Tasmanian devil in overdrive. And I'm too impulsive. Something pops into my head and I act on it without thinking it through first. I can't hold down a job, no matter what it is. I don't have any money, not matter how much I try to save. I never get laid. I'm lonely. I'm ugly. Nobody loves me. I have no prospects or talent. What I'm trying to say is I'm no good. I'm nothing. Oddly enough I'm not suicidal. Still, my life is a stand up routine. What am I gonna do? I can't afford to be out of work for another hour."

Dale hated throwing pity parties. They made him uncomfortable to the point of hysteria. So he pretended that his friend wasn't there. He glanced around his cubapt with a confused expression, as if he might have heard somebody say something but wasn't sure.

"Dale?" said Achtung 66.799.

Dale opened up a window and stuck out his head. "Who said that? How do you know my name? Answer me!"

Before leaving, Achtung 66.799 filled up a test tube with Sea Monkey powder, added the appropriate chemicals, watched the creatures sprout into existence, and fried them over the Bunsen burner.

Depression. His body hung limply from his jetpack on the flight home. He couldn't remember feeling worse. Maybe he was suicidal after all. Killing himself would certainly solve his problems. He would be doing the jampacked world a favor, ridding it of an excess body. Plus he would ease his parents' consciences; in the wake of his death, they no longer had to worry about him being an irretrievable failure. All he had to do was unbuckle his jetpack and he would plummet into the trellis of flyways beneath him where an engine or propeller or wingblade would rip him to shreds. It would be quick, easy. And morally commendable. He owed it to the world to kill himself. By not killing himself, he was doing the world a disservice as he contributed absolutely nothing to civilization and the betterment of humanity. He had no excuse for not committing suicide. The very thought of allowing himself to live repulsed him...

He came to a sharp halt. An alaristrian had been riding his ass and smashed into him. His jetpack stalled and he swore at Achtung 66.799 as he sunk like an anchor, trying to get the engine started again. Achtung 66.799 whispered a halfhearted apology and quickly ducked off the flyway. Hovering in the air, he stared doggedly at the advertisement on the vidbuilding across the street.

HONOR! VALOR! FATALITY!

ARE YOU IN THE MOOD FOR BEING SECOND TO NONE?

NO BETTER FRIEND, NO WORSE ENEMY

SEMPER FEE-FIE-FOE-FUM...

I SMELL THE BLOOD OF AN EVERYMAN

BECOME THE ARM OF DECISION

BECOME HELL IN A HANDCAMERA

JOIN TODAY!

Beneath the script was the gigantic image of a smiling head distinguished by an anvil chin, a Picadilly bouffant hairdo, and two surgically altered animé eyes. Achtung 66.799 slipped into a trance. He had seen similar advertisements before. Tens of thousands of them on tens of thousands of occasions. But only now, as he stood on the doorstep of self-annihilation, did it command his attention. All his life, the idea of becoming "second to none" had been inconceivable. Not only was it generally considered to be the absolute lowest, most despicable form of employment (despite the fact that its workerbees were ubiquitous), his father had always threatened to disown him if he joined, claiming that the life of a serial killer or plaquedemic would be a more respectable fate. That didn't matter now. Better to be alive and working than dead and useless. Not in his father's eyes, but he never really liked his father anyway. And in the end he was far too afraid of death to kill himself.

In less than an hour, Achtung 66.799 stood in a line that ran halfway across Bliptown, enjoying his soon-to-be-flushed-down-the-toilet identity and reflecting on the vagaries of his short career as a dysfunctional postcapitalist...

Achtung 66.799's experience wasn't unique. His perpetual failure as a functional postcapitalist was in fact the definition of contemporary normalcy. The yellow brick road he skipped down had been stained with multitudes of muddy footprints centuries before he came along. And they all led to the same place.

The legion. The proud.

The Papanazi.

As in the former military, anybody could join. Years ago it had been required by Law to serve in the Papanazi at some point between the ages of 20-28 for at least three years. Nowadays service was optional. Nonetheless thousands flocked to the profession daily. No education was required—graduate, postgraduate or otherwise. One only needed a semi-serviceable brain and a downright fascist willingness to covet imagery at the expense of pride, morality, ideology, and life.

The industry was dangerously popular. Papanazi soldiers outnumbered other non-Papanazi people two and a half to one. Each stood to make a million, but 99.999 percent were tier 26 neobourgeois proles in terms of income. This perturbed and pathologized more than a few Papanazi, but not as much as what was known as The Terminal Stipulation, which dictated that Papanaziism was the only profession in which workers could not surrogate themselves with androids. While they were difficult to monitor in light of the Papanazi's vast numbers, offenders faced the maximum degree of the Law's absurd wrath.

Prior to walking into the Department of Mediatization, Achtung 66.799 had owned a different name. It was wiped from his memory. Every now and then the name's ghost came back to haunt him, but even the most inept sideshow exorcists had little trouble getting rid of it. For the most part Achtung 66.799's makeshift, massified identity was perfectly stable. Stable or unstable, though, anybody could shoot a celebrity.

Dr. Identity

There was a new celebrity in town. Two of them, and they had become megastars in record fasttime. Achtung 66.799 was filled with hope when he heard the news. Feelings of hope also welled up in Achtung 66.800, Achtung 204.111, Achtung 4.003, Achtung 56.309, Achtung 3,983.145, Achtung 51.582, Achtung 366.472, Achtung 77.340, Achtung 77.341, Achtung 77.342, Achtung 7,342.342, Achtung 1.001, Achtung 344.822, Achtung 8,196.342, Achtung 99.999, Achtung 999.999, Achtung 9,999.999, Achtung 99,999.999...

07
littleoldladyville, part 2 – 1ˢᵗ person ('blah)

"I want my old name back." I flicked a ladybug off the sleeve of my golf shirt. "No reason to call myself ——— anymore. No reason to call myself doctor or professor anymore, for that matter."

Dr. Identity stood on his tip-toes and removed a fetus from the shelf. The fetus was floating in a smart Güntergrass bottle of formaldehyde. "What about Blah Blah Blah?"

"That's not funny."

"It's funny." Dr. Identity examined the apparently female fetus, concentrating on the shriveled umbilical cord that spiraled from its navel like a rotten pigtail. The android's pupils dilated as they zoomed in and out. "I don't believe I even know what your real name is. Not that it really matters to me. Names are mere signs. They have nothing to do with the bodies they signify and are forcibly connected to."

"What are you, Ferdinand de Saussure? I don't need a lesson in structuralism. I need a lesson in how to achieve agency from a crazy fucking 'gänger."

Dr. Identity said, "This piece is fantastic. A vintage fetus. They don't make them like this anymore. What's it doing in the speculative weapons department?"

The fetus opened its eyes and mouthed the words HELP ME. I said, "What the hell is formaldehyde anyway? I have no idea. I wonder if you can drink it and live."

Dr. Identity placed the fetus back on the shelf and removed a shockstick nunchaku. "I can. I can drink hot lava." It sized up the weapon, palming and gauging its weight. "I recall one occasion when a student-thing thought he might play a joke on me by offering me a drink from a thermos full of hot lava he smuggled into class. He passed the substance off as a hip brand of coffee. Sipperella 007 if memory serves. I suppose he thought my jaw would melt." It leisurely began to fling the nunchaku through the loopholes of its body. "The lava actually tasted all right. I guzzled the whole thermos. Then I burped in the student-thing's face and singed off his unibrow."

I looked awry at Dr. Identity. "Anyway, I'm going back to my original name."

"Good for you. Good for you." The nunchaku accelerated. "What's your name again?"

I opened my mouth to respond...and realized I had no response. I had forgotten my original name.

Dr. Identity smirked. "I see."

I was infuriated. And vaguely nauseous. I had only given the name up a year and a half ago. How could I have already forgotten it? "I'm sure I have it written down somewhere," I said helplessly. I felt like smashing something.

The nunchaku moved so quickly I couldn't see them. Nor could I see my 'gänger's arms. "Don't worry about it. You'll remember your name. Right now there's more pressing matters at hand, yes? Weapons and disguises. And a bit of food, of course. Weapons first, though, weapons first." Abruptly it stopped wielding the nunchaku and returned them to the shelf. "Too heavy. And I honestly prefer swords. They're more to the point, if you'll excuse the wordplay. We'll need guns, too. Lots of guns."

"How do you plan to carry all of this goddamn artillery?" My ailing memory harrowed me. Frantic, I pawed through its murky depths, searching for my identity...

Dr. Identity shook its head and pointed at its crotch. "We've got enough space between us in here to carry a small army—literally. The pockets in these pants are de la Footwa's Black Holes. Didn't you know? It's my understanding that Beesuppies are delivered into existence readymade with de la Footwa's sewn in their dress pants. They've got a lot to hide, after all. You might want to check your pockets. On the way over here I found a few questionable objects in mine."

De la Footwa's Black Holes. I'd heard of them. But I'd never really believed in them, if for nothing else than they were far too expensive to afford on a plaquedemic's salary, no matter how distinguished you were in the Biz. According to their inventor, Jean-Claude Baudelaire Hillary Wapakoneta de la Footwa, they were inspired by an old cartoon show called *Henri Hackensack* starring a German "curt jester" of the same name who had a bad habit of arbitrarily pulling entire alternate realities out of his navel. The pockets molecularized all material objects you put inside of them, and when you took the objects out, the pockets molarized them back to their original form. Some versions even had room for psychic storage in the event that a wearer experienced an overload of schizophrenic personalities, a common experience in Bliptown. In fact, I discovered a discarded personality when I reached into one of the pockets. I gripped it by the mane and pulled it out. It looked like Benito Mussolini with its big head and commanding overlip, only after the Italian tyrant had been executed: one side of its face was melted off and there were gaping bullet holes in its chest. The personality shouted something in Schizospeak and ran off. Other items I removed from my pockets included a leatherbound steering wheel, a tennis racket, a set of golf clubs, a briefcase (full of Saltines and miniature packages of peanut butter), a file drawer (full of dirty vidzines), and the corpses of two dogs, one a bloodhound, the other a teacup Yorkshire terrier. All of this baggage was filthy, stained in blood and dirt, and slick with ectoplasm. I tossed the items on the floor one by one.

A trashcan standing at attention on the ledge of a catwalk four stories above us caught sight of the mess. It dove off of its perch, jetted down to Dr. Identity and me, devoured and digested the contents of the Beesuppie's pockets in one great vaporizing inhale, scolded me for being a litterbug, informed us that it had been watching our movements, warned us that we only had a few minutes left before being found guilty of not buying anything, and finally disappeared into a trap door that suddenly opened beneath it.

I looked at Dr. Identity.

"Don't give me that look. I didn't do anything to deserve that look."

I raised my voice. "You didn't do anything? Are you kidding me?"

"Yes. Let's get to work." Cool and businesslike, it started taking weapons off the shelves and shoving them into its pockets. Its movements fell somewhere between realtime and fasttime. Whenever a weapon vanished into the obscurity of the android's pockets, it fizzled out in a puff of holographic sparks. "Not much time to waste," it added without pausing. "I sense a shitstorm about to break."

Traffic in the aisle was nominal. Just a few grandmothers snailing here and there interrupted by the occasional wolfpack of teenagers. Nobody minded anything but themselves and their shopperly duties. But that didn't matter. The Babettas were what we had to worry about. And the Bug-Eyed Monsters. Despite the speed with which it played thief, Dr. Identity was in all likelihood already being clocked by some extension of Littleoldladyville's surveillance system. It was only a matter of seconds before the proverbial dogs were set on us.

I tried to map out how things would go down. I had a little fighting experience and knew how to swing a blade—like most boys, I spent virtually all of my early adolescent spare time scikungfi swordfighting in the Schizoverse. I could handle a gun, too. Shortly after I was born, my mother-thing developed an addiction to firearms, a condition provoked by one of her boyfriends. He was a door-to-door plasma gun salesman. She took me to a shooting gallery before I was old enough to speak, and as far back as my memory carried me, our cubapt looked more like an arsenal than a place to live. I hadn't so much as picked up a gun since my mother-thing died eight years ago. Even if I had, I wouldn't be able to fend off the collective wrath of whatever mindless contraptions were sicced on me. Not with any type of weaponry. Not even with

Dr. Identity, who had proved itself to be an effective (albeit psychotic) war machine. In other words, I fully expected to die within the next few minutes. Who was I kidding? I was as adept with a sword and a gun as I was negotiating the feelings and complaints of ornery student-things. I wondered how Skyler Buhbye, the protagonist of *Technofetahshit Salad*, a neurorealistic novel I taught last semester, would have felt in my shoes. I wondered how I felt for that matter: at that particular moment I couldn't determine whether I was frightened beyond recognition, hopelessly apathetic, or helplessly euphoric.

A line from a Hardy Boys novel came to me: *The boys leapt into the red convertible like handfuls of loose change...*

I walked down the aisle and removed a plague sword from the shelf. It was light, thin, the color of TV static. Impossibly sharp. I could almost feel it slicing through my gaze as I looked it over.

I thrust the sword into my pocket. A plume of cold sparks tickled the skin of my hand.

I collected more weapons, trying to catch Dr. Identity. I loaded up on guns, ammunition, swords, entropics. I was especially attracted to coagulators. In many of the science fiction texts I taught, coagulators were fearsome biological weapons. They inflicted damage to living body tissue, rearranging and scrambling one's musculature, nervous system, and internal organs in hideous ways.

The pockets were extremely user-friendly. No sense of weight at all in my britches. The more I filled them up, in fact, the lighter they seemed to become. I started to feel like I might float away.

I didn't know how much time passed before it began. As little as fifteen seconds. As much as two minutes. Probably closer to fifteen seconds—any longer and a BEM would at least have us in its sights.

One moment I was grabbing speculative weapons. The next I was the centerpiece in a montage of gore and ultraviolence.

I blacked out...

Dr. Identity told me about the skirmish later. We were sitting in a bratwurst bar, sipping cognac and eating pâté. "What do you remember?" it asked.

"Nothing. Nothing."

"Nothing twice over. Hmm. Well. We looked good. Our disguises were state-of-the-art. But that didn't stop the Babettas. Or the Bug-Eyed Monsters."

Not coincidentally, they looked exactly like aliens who belonged to the universe of pulp science fiction. Each BEM had been patterned after a creature illustrated on the cover of an early issue of *Amazing Stories*, a twentieth century pulp science fiction magazine whose founder and editor, Hugo Gernsback, had in recent years been retrospectively held accountable for the terminal depthlessness of the film industry. The bulk of the BEM's body, of course, consisted of two gigantic, greasy eyes. Its other prominent features included shark's teeth, long crablike pincers, and a scorpion's tail fully loaded with venDom, a substance that, once injected, literally turned victims into commodities, rearranging their molecular structure so that they metabolically devolved into the product they had purchased most frequently at Littleoldladyville. Hilda Grumpstead was an avid reader of *Amazing Stories* as a little girl, even though the magazine had long been out of print, and this particular BEM terrified her. Hence she recruited it as her scarecrow and executioner.

I would have never survived on my own.

Dr. Identity told me how it played offense and defense for both of us. I stood there dumbly.

The first BEM galloped towards me, snorting like a rhinoceros. Veins popped out of the great whites of its eyes. Its tail loomed above its grotesque head. The BEM's stinger was a drooling vampire's mouth complete with blood red lips and fangs.

"You reminded me of a crash test dummy I once knew," Dr. Identity remarked. "I've scarcely witnessed such passivity before in the line of fire, especially from a human. My my my." It removed a bratwurst ball from the tower of hors d'oeuvres that a stickbot with a gondolier mustache set down in front of us. It examined the ball apprehensively...

Dr. Identity took out the BEM, hacking off its tail with a swarm sword and then driving the blade between its eyes. The BEM's body twitched as if electrocuted. The vampire mouth of its tail cursed in an extinct Romanian dialect.

I stood there dumbly.

The razorsharp spidersteel bees that constituted the swarm sword melted out of formation and, at Dr. Identity's behest, projected towards two more attacking BEMs.

Dr. Identity yanked a superchilled scythe out of its pocket. It leapt ten feet in the air and came down on another BEM like a sledgehammer, spearing it with the commanding fluidity of a matador. Dr. Identity became one with the alien— its arm, its shoulder, its cheek pressed against a clammy eye. The BEM froze from the inside out. Dr. Identity stomped on its head and shattered it. Adopting the full-fledged stance of a matador now, my 'gänger conjured a red cape and exhibited a series of graceful veronicas as BEMs charged us. He finished each of them off quickly and somewhat cleanly with a different brand of technosword, then pulled out a sawed off ray gun and incinerated an entire herd.

"I must have taken out forty, fifty of those bastards," Dr. Identity explained, half-drunk now from the cognac. "Then things really started to get hairy."

Melodrome played constantly in Littleoldladyville. Different departments featured different pieces. The sporting goods department, for instance, played instrumental renditions of old Boxcar Willie songs like "Mule Train" and "Polly Wolly Doodle," whereas sleeker, neobourgeois renditions of more recent artists' work piped into the hairware department. As it barraged consumers with a perpetual flow of subliminal messages encouraging them to shop with more and more gusto, Melodrome reflected the process of consumption. When mass shopping sprees broke out, it accelerated and became more strident, representing the mania of so many furious transactions taking place at once; when shopping droughts occurred, it flowed with turtlelike sluggishness.

There were few if any transactions taking place in the speculative weapons department. For whatever reason, the Melodrome treated the brawl like a consumer's apocalypse, mirroring the ebb and flow of the ultraviolence.

Most of the shoppers in the aisle had fled. A few shoppers had been peripherally mauled by a BEM or Dr. Identity; incapacitated, they studied and clutched their wounds. All of the BEMs had been destroyed or rendered inoperable. A junkyard of machinery surrounded us.

My idiocy knew no end. I continued to behave like a stone tablet, physically and psychologically. Despite myself, however, I was never in any real danger. Every BEM that locked on me was slain before its tail had the chance to sink its fangs into my flesh. I emerged without a scratch.

Then the Babettas fell. The Melodrome surged as they rained from the labyrinthine electric sky of Littleoldladyville.

There were hundreds of them. "Four hundred and forty-six," Dr. Identity bragged.

Somewhere in the neon maze of catwalks, spiral escalators, chutes and ladders above us must have been a storage facility. I had no idea so many Babettas even existed in one place.

Regiment after regiment swan dove to the floor on bungee cords, then sprung backwards onto high heels and assumed various scikungfi stances. Accompanying the old bags were a few gangs of bounty hunters and professional vigilantes summoned by the fasttime imagery of the Papanazi to avenge and capitalize on the death of Voss Winkenweirder. So far only a handful of Papanazis loomed overhead. But that was enough. One would have been enough. They hung above us like light fixtures, suspended in the air by propeller beanies, filming the scene with their technologized gazes.

Dr. Identity admitted to feeling momentarily overwhelmed. So much so that he punched me out and stuffed me into the hollowed out corpse of a BEM. "I'm sorry, friend. I concluded at that point that you were more of a burden than a boon. This had been the case all along, of course, but I didn't want to injure your already ailing morale."

"That's nice."

"Trust me. You didn't want to have anything to do with consciousness. There were little old ladies running around on stilts for goddsakes. Stilts!

I don't like stilts. I harbor an irrational fear of them. And they serve no real purpose outside of a circus." It set down the bratwurst ball it had been inspecting, picked up another one, and popped it into its mouth without hesitation.

I finished my cognac and ordered a shot of tequila from a stickbot wearing an oversized beret that made it look more like a hat rack than an emaciated French waiter. "Tout suite!" it exclaimed. Another exclamation followed, this one from a man sitting at a nearby table who was apparently excited about using the restroom. "I can't wait to get my ass on that toilet!" he told his wife-thing and hurried off.

"I wish everybody would calm down," I said disgustedly. "This fucking enthusiasm is killing me."

Dr. Identity shook its head. "A little enthusiasm never hurt anyone." It scratched its chin. "Actually that's not true. Enthusiasm is essentially a product of the adrenal glands, and adrenaline leads to all kinds of preposterous havoc. It makes sense. Adrenaline exists in the human body as a safeguard against dangerous phenomena, or rather what's perceived to be dangerous phenomena. I lack the juice myself, but then again I don't need it, do I. In any event, those Babettas were 'on the rag,' as it were. The only weapons they used were their claws and the occasional set of brass knuckles. Had I been of lesser mettle, they would have trounced me. But I made quick work of them. I made quick work of all our attackers, especially the Papanazis. All this in spite of your initial skepticism. I don't know why you continue to doubt my skills: you programmed me. It's not my fault you programmed me to be the physical, intellectual and ideological superhero you've wanted to be since you read your first comic book. You should have seen the mess I left behind. Littleoldladyville was a steaming landfill of carcasses and car parts when we jetpacked out of there. But we made it, and with plenty of booty, I might add. We have enough designer disguises to last more than a few lifetimes, not to mention the refrigerators full of food and drink that Jean-Claude Baudelaire Hillary Wapakoneta de la Footwa permitted us to stash away. It certainly is fun to be an übermensch. You should try it sometime."

Ignoring Dr. Identity's ever-increasing megalomania, I said, "Women that old can't menstruate. Most women go through menopause in their seventies or eighties. Babettas were patterned after a 140-year-old woman."

Dr. Identity's facemask altered slightly when he frowned—a mustache popped onto his overlip and his chin sharpened. "I don't understand."

"The Babettas couldn't have been 'on the rag,' as you say, because they're too goddamn old."

"But they're machines."

"Precisely."

"I still don't understand."

"I don't understand why you still don't understand. 'On the rag' is an improper use of language. The colloquialism doesn't function in the context you use it in."

"It's just an expression. What does context have to do with an expression's metaphorical impact?"

"Jesus. Forget it." But I couldn't let it go. "Look. What I'm saying is—"

The distant, familiar bark of DNA hounds interrupted me. The bratwurst bar was located on the 12,302½th floor of an anonymous spacescraper that stood on the outer limits of one of Bliptown's many French-Canadian quarters. The sky outside the futique Venetian windows of the bar grew darker as the barking grew louder and patrons glanced querulously over their shoulders.

"Cunt on a stick. We have to get our DNA reconfigured." I stood and wiped my mouth. "I'm tired of running around like a couple of assholes."

Dr. Identity smiled politely at a patron who looked in our direction. "Don't be silly. There's only one asshole in this relationship." It stood up and rearranged its cuff links and ear lobes. "Just kidding. Anyway I'm enjoying the challenge of being on the lam. Actually it's not much of a challenge. But it's interesting. It's certainly more interesting than trying to teach student-things how to read and not act like amoebas. In spite of your nagging moral conundrum, you must admit this simplistic truth."

"No more holocausts," I said, pointing at Dr. Identity with an admonitory finger. "Ultraviolence is for the weak."

"Not if you commit it with flair. Not if you turn it into poetry. That's the nature of the future."

"Poetry died with the modernists. T.S. Eliot was the last real poet."

"I agree!" said the man sitting next to us to his wife-thing after a period of intense deliberation. He wasn't talking about my assertion. He was talking about the taste of a lemon cookie, which the wife-thing had casually remarked was delicious.

Dr. Identity pressed a sensor in the middle of its chest. A streamlined, platinum-plated, single-engine jet unfolded out of the crease in the back of its Beethoven blazer. Barely visible, the machine was the most expensive, efficient model on the market: the Bobafett 4001. It would very likely remain the most expensive, efficient model for another two, possibly three weeks, an unheard of length of time in Type 1 countries. "Nobody's going to die today," Dr. Identity announced so that the entire bratwurst bar could hear. Its facemask was sentient and telepathic. It told the facemask to take the form of its actual visage. "That's a promise from me, Dr. Identity, to all of you."

"Shit." I fired up my own Bobafett 4001. "Get rid of your face, goddamn you." I could see the DNA hounds outside the window now. They were reconstructions of the mythological Cerberus with the exceptions of caricatured human noses and vast pterodactyl wings. They flapped towards the bar at ramming speed.

On our way out, the 'gänger of a fan asked Dr. Identity for its autograph, pulling out a synthetic triple-D breast and handing it a needle. Dr. Identity's pupils morphed into stiff exclamation points as it inscribed its name in an impeccable cursive font around a perfectly circular, perfectly hard nipple.

The 'gänger's owner, in turn, asked for my autograph, assuming I was Dr. Identity's sidekick regardless of my facemask. I didn't know what made me refuse her more: Time's winged chariot hurrying near, my merciless inability to remember my real name, or the fact that she handed me a pen and paper.

08
the wife-thing & other minutia – 3ʳᵈ person

On a skyscreen situated between the Slipslide Interpass and the Rigor Mortis Flyway, a commercial for a new and improved brand of prosthetic genitals dissolved into the digitized headshot of Anchorman Dominique Erstwhile. His face was a great white smile atop which sat two grafted lobster eyeballs and a sculpted Yabbadabba hairdo.

"Plaquedemics!" he exclaimed. The camera cut to an enormous amphitheater full of movie-goers who responded to the exclamation with a communal tsunamic shriek...

The camera cut back to Anchorman Erstwhile. "Good morning, citizens," he intoned in a flawlessly articulated, freakishly resonant monotone. "The doctors have struck again. The havoc they have wreaked over the past few hours has been monstrous, devastating, evil, and downright unsportsmanlike. What kind of fucking shitheads are these assholes? FOXXX Channel 7,934 Newsman Bing Dingaling is at the home of Dr. ——— and his wife-thing to field this very question. Bing?"

Traffic near the skyscreen screeched to an impossible halt and hovered silently in the flyways...

Wide view of a fat, plaid loveseat positioned in front of a kitchenette. Out-of-date wallpaper. Pastiche of miniature cabinets and appliances...Police Pigs rummaged through the cabinets with razorsnouts, throwing cups and plates and silverware over their shoulders. Their projectile eyes were the objective lenses of high-powered microscopes. Two Pigs tore off a refrigerator door and leapt inside. Another Pig sat on the couch next to Dr. ———'s wife-thing. Her hair was an abandoned bird's nest. Dried tributaries of mascara described her sallow cheeks. A tattered Billingsley dress hung over her undernourished although not ill-built frame.

The Pig perched on the loveseat like a little boy in the waiting room of a doctor's office, its rear hooves barely hanging over the edge while one of its frontal hooves crept up the wife-thing's thigh.

As the hoof neared its mark, the Pig turned to the wife-thing and asked her a series of rapidfire questions in Squealspeak.

She stared into the camera with her mouth half open.

Newsman Dingaling's head rose onto the skyscreen, blocking the action behind it.

"Thank you, Dominique," said the head. It was a smooth, square head that looked sculpted out of clay. The skin was bronze and moisturized. Matching dimples had been implanted into the tip of the chin and nose. Wingtip Wizard-of-Oz eyebrows had been grafted onto the forehead. "I'm here at the cubapt of Dr. ———, villain, fiend, homewrecker, and, as Dominique so accurately put it, fucking shithead. The plaquedemic and his 'gänger have been at large since this morning's preliminary holocaust at Corndog University. At the moment they have perpetrated twelve additional holocausts, one of which involved the tragic death of Voss Winkenweirder. The loss of this national icon has incited virtually every destructive emotion in the collective consciousness of the science fictionalized world."

A montage of clips from Voss Winkenweirder's ultraviolent scikungfi films flashed across the skyscreen.

"Winkenweirder's 'gänger, Victor Bleep, is reported to have mortally short-circuited upon hearing news of the celebrity's death. No news as of yet when, if ever, it will be able to resume the shooting of the late great movie star's current project, *Finger Lickin' Fürher*, based on the dream life of the rapper of the same name."

A medley of Squealspeak blasphemes exploded behind Bing Dingaling.

His head rotated 180 degrees as if on a turntable. Meticulously shaved into the back of his Hangman hairdo was an advertisement for a new brand of designer nostrils. The advertisement promised an inconceivable sniffing experience.

Dingaling sized up the commotion and his head rotated back into place. One lip corner curled up as if yanked by a fish hook. "The motive for these seemingly random acts of ultraviolence is still unclear, but the Papanazi is on the case, and in due course the truth will inevitably be uncovered and revealed. Whatever the truth turns out to be, however, experts agree that there is simply no excuse for these repeated public displays of yobbery. I'm here at Dr. ——— —'s residence in an attempt to get a better sense of what makes this satanic plaquedemic and his mechanical henchman tick."

Boggle-eyed, Dingaling stepped back from the camera, exposing the cubapt again. The Pigs had gone. Dr. ———'s wife-thing lay spread out on the couch. One of her breasts hung free. Her mouth was a twisted hole. A family of cybernetic flies circled her.

The newsman told her to put her breast away and scoot over. She didn't hear him. He pardoned himself, took hold of the breast, squeezed and tested its resilience, smirked at the camera, returned the breast to its casing, pushed the wife-thing's body to one side of the couch, and sat down next to her.

He smirked at the camera again. "Good afternoon, Mrs. ———. Thank you for taking the time to meet with us. That's a lovely dress you're wearing. Is it edible? I'm tempted to make a meal out of it." He tipped a microphone shaped like a dildo to her mouth.

The wife-thing blinked.

"Well then," said Dingaling, "I'll get right to the dirty little point. What can you tell us about that son of a bitch husband of yours? Why is he acting like such a bastard? What can you tell us about his 'gänger, Dr. Identity? Did Dr. ——— consciously program a mass murderer? Have you ever even met Dr. Identity? How many times a week do you have sex with your husband? What is his favorite position? How long is his penis? Is Dr. Identity equipped with a penis? If so, is it operational? Were you having an affair with your husband's 'gänger? Do you have a 'gänger? If so, does it have nipples and a vagina? Are you a hermaphrodite? What are you hiding? Have you ever eaten poi? Do you have any illicit piercings, tattoos, or prosthetics? Have you ever used the word *usufruct* in casual conversation? Do you shave your pubic hair into funny shapes? Do you think plaquedemia has any use-value whatsoever? Are you proud to be the wife-thing of a wanted plaquedemic? Would you allow me to French kiss you if I asked politely? Tell us, Mrs. ———, why are you being so difficult? Why are you so reticent to discuss the lives of two criminals who are clearly possessed by the Devil?"

Bing Dingaling paused. The volley of questions had been served in one giant breath. Fatigued and dizzy, he placed his elbows on his knees, leaned over, and breathed deeply into a wrinkled up paper bag. The camera slowly zoomed in on the wife-thing, pining for a response→→→→her mouth creaked open, slowly, very slowly, and fixed itself into a frozen, silent scream. The camera moved closer→→→→closer and closer→→→→until the most prominent feature on the skyscreen was her epiglottis, glistening like an udder dipped ·in honey. Tattooed onto the body of the epiglottis was an intricate zebra pattern reminiscent of a pattern produced by Blackie Colecovision, this week's wealthiest fashion designer. Some of the viewers wondered if the tattoo was permanent or temporary and if the pattern was authentic or counterfeit. One viewer wondered if she was born that way...

The camera snapped back to its original position.

Bing Dingaling had regained composure, although his eyebrows looked like roadkill. He sensed the anomalies and quickly smoothed them out. "Aren't we Mrs. Chatty Chatty Bang Bang-thing," he baritoned, and pressed his nose. A short, metallic laugh track sounded off. Dingaling laughed with it, locking round, wide eyes with the camera, which zoomed in on him→→→→and froze. The laugh track squeaked silent. Bing Dingaling's open mouth collapsed into a pleasant smile. The smile was recognizably Wolfsschanzian, a vintage piece worth more than his Critchlow flybike. He also owned a Wolfsschanzian frown, but he hardly ever used it, even when he wasn't on camera; not only was the frown invaluable, his permit had expired and he kept forgetting to renew it. The minimum penalty for sporting an expired, patented facial gesture was twenty minutes in a rainforest: more than enough time to die.

"Critics have been debating the stimulus for this understandably distraught wife-thing's bitter half," the newsman whirred. "Most popular is the belief that his actions are a psychosomatic reaction to being a plaquedemic, the most despised profession in the postcapitalist universe aside from the door-to-door salesman, which, following the downfall of linguistic cyberspace, has come back into prominence. It is also believed that this reaction was exacerbated by the fact that Dr. ——— is a *mediocre* plaquedemic who is not only hated by ordinary people but by his colleagues as well. Plaquedemics gauge their absurdist worth based upon the publication of literary criticism and theory. If they don't publish a certain quantity of articles, essays or books in venues that are deemed appropriate by their parliament, the Ministry of Stoutfellow, they are encouraged to be shamed, berated, and more or less treated like turds by their co-workers. As is well-known, teaching skills ceased to be a plaquedemic requirement long ago. The plaquedemic doesn't need to know how to teach, only to write publishable criticism on irrelevant issues that nobody has the intellectual capacity to read, process, interpret and apply to daily life. Dr. ——— —'s track record is a sad affair. He has published next to nothing. What little he has published appeared in journals that the Ministry of Stoutfellow declared 'far less than noteworthy.' I happened to read one of these publications. It was an article called 'The Post(post)/post-post+postmodern Icklyophobe: Ultra/counter\hypernihilism in Fiona Birdwater's megaanti-micronovel, *The Ypsilanti Factor*.' God only knows what this goddamned essay is about. God only knows what any goddamned plaquedemic essay is about. Nonetheless even I could tell that Dr. ———'s writing was far below Stoutfellow standards. That said, I have gas. I have to use the toilet. Be back in a flash. Excuse me."

Abruptly Bing Dingaling stood and waltzed offscreen, leaving the wife-thing there to endure the fervent stare of the camera. She didn't endure it well. Her agitated face seemed to be falling apart and rebuilding itself at the same time. The camera quickly became bored with this physiognomic spectacle and zoomed into her breasts→→→→which spilled onto her blouse like overturned buckets of mud.

Viewers in the flyways squinted at the skyscreen, unsure of the authenticity of the breasts...

Eventually the scene cut to a schizercial. A pyrotechnic tableau of subliminal image-bursts permeated the skyscreen and downloaded themselves into viewers' unconsciouses, all of them competing for pole position on the mental racetrack of consumer desire.

Three and a half minutes later the schizercial faded back into Dr. ———'s cubapt. The wife-thing exhibited the same frenetic expression as before. Bing Dingaling's head was buried underneath her dress. Kneeling on the couch, his ass waved back and forth as he attended to her private part.

Sensing the camera's gaze, he pulled his head into the open and sat upright. "Nope," he said tersely, smoothing back his hair, "I didn't lose my lunchbox down there after all." He pressed his nose. The laugh track blared, silenced...Dingaling grinned. "Now then, Mrs. ———, we were discussing the degraded condition of the plaquedemic, e.g., your husband, yes?" He pulled a handkerchief out of his breast pocket and dabbed the corners of his wet lips. He tossed the handkerchief over his shoulder. "You mentioned something about your husband being an embarrassment to Stoutfellowhood, not to mention mankind, if I'm not mistaken. Am I mistaken?" Dingaling glanced at the wife-thing expectantly.

The wife-thing's eyes rolled back into her head. She burped and said something inaudible before slumping onto the armrest of the couch.

Dingaling looked at the camera. "Many critics have debated whether or not Dr. ——— and his technological extension Dr. Identity would have turned out to be such sons of bitches if the professor had lived up to the caliber of his mentor, the illustrious Dr. Hugo Saxony Hamsalad, winner of two Pulitzer Prizes, one for a greeting card, the other for a grocery list. Upon hearing the news of his protégé's fall from disgrace, Dr. Hamsalad was said to be as 'bereft' as he was 'beguiled.'"

The camera flashcut to a close-up headshot of Dr. Hamsalad. His face was severely gaunt but somehow strong, like a bodybuilding cancer patient. *Mal vogue* pince-nez sat on the bulb of his nose. Bushy handlebar sideburns dwarfed the ruff of silver hair on his forehead. "I am as bereft as I am beguiled," the professor said in a machinic staccato. "I knew my protégé was a bad egg all along. I remember one occasion in particular. The young scoundrel was—"

A giant hook curled around Dr. Hamsalad's neck and yanked him off camera.

Back to Dingaling. "Spoken like a true plaquedemic. Thank you, sir." He cleared a ball of phlegm from his throat and spit it out. He smiled. "As I was saying, Dr. —— is a no-good fiend. The acts of ultraviolence he and his 'gänger have committed belong to the Schizoverse, not to the real world. He is obviously a deeply disturbed human being. More than a few pundits have argued that the reason for such reckless behavior is that Dr. —— actually believes he is inhabiting the Schizoverse. Others argue that he is an evil-intentioned alien disguised as a human. Some say he is a professional Norman Bates impersonator with a mean-on. Your thoughts, Mrs. ——?" Dingaling leaned over and knocked on her temple with the microphone.

The wife-thing snorted awake. She glanced stupidly around the room and ordered a chocolate chip mint-flavored ice cream cone in a little girl's voice. Dingaling pushed out his lips. The wife-thing stood up, fainted, and fell backwards over the couch with a crash of pots and pans.

Dingaling glanced over the couch, then back at the camera. "Whatever Dr. ——'s condition, his behavior clearly stems from some kind of prepubescent trauma. A biography of his early life is currently being written. It is expected to be published later this week. Film rights have been secured as well. On board so far are Stanley Ashenbach as Dr. Identity, John Jacob Jingleheimer Rabinowitz as Dr. ——, Sindie Switch as his wife-thing, Daria Crazyeight as his white trash mistress, and Bavarian Frank and Magdelene Underoos as his bleached white trash parent-things. I have been asked to play the role of myself. The film is tentatively being called *The Dystopian Duo*. Look for it in theaters the week after next. Back to you, Dominique."

"Munnk ooo erkl furdrib nurf," Anchorman Erstwhile mumbled. He set aside a Ten Story sandwich and quickly chewed and swallowed the gigantic bite in his mouth. He belched. "Pardon me. Thank you, Bing. Stay tuned to FOXXX Channel 7,934 for the most up-to-date information on Bliptown's Warlords of Wickedness. We leave you with a look at the Winkenweirder camp, where the celebrity's people have been mourning his death like rockstars. I'm Dominique Erstwhile."

Long range telescopic view of a sprawling rooftop estate. The family and friends of the movie star darted in and out of doors, in and out of windows, in and out of pools like headless chickens. Piles of empty bottles and hypodermic needles everywhere. Some mourners sobbed uncontrollably. Some were passed out. Some were naked and on all fours, growling and howling and clawing at the air. A buzzing cumulonimbus cloud of Papanazi in jetpacks and propeller hats loomed above the estate. Every few seconds one of them dove down from the cloud to get a closer shot of the spectacle of grief.

09
in the hall of the mountain kings – 3ʳᵈ person

Mr. Horace Q. Whackbottom was late again. He had been seeing his third string mistress' 'gänger on the sly. Nothing got him off in bed like a good old-fashioned dirty mouth, and the android's mouth was much dirtier than its owner's. Sometimes his mistress sent the 'gänger to visit him in her stead, and vice versa. No problem. But she had no idea it had been sneaking away without permission to fool around with her patron for almost a year now. It wasn't the 'gänger's fault. One night Mr. Whackbottom reprogrammed it to desire him *in extremis*. A sexogenetically enhanced older gentleman, he met her at least once a day in random places: public toilets, janitor's closets, stock rooms, tanning booths, vidphone booths, walk-in cryogenic freeze chambers, treetops, jumping gyms... Today he had scheduled it to meet him in an out-of-the-way revolving door located in the basement of his office spacescraper, but the android didn't show up. The door was a sentient, always-be-turning apparatus, and as he stepped in slow circles around its mirrored base, he implored it to talk dirty to him.

"Profanity is not part of my lexicon," the door replied.

Mr. Whackbottom raised an eyebrow. "Oh? I can rectify that problem."

"Please, sir. Behave yourself."

"Lick my asshole."

Finally Mr. Whackbottom stepped out of the door. He had been waiting and revolving for over twenty minutes. Woozy, his vision spotted. He tipped over and passed out.

He woke up. Stood up. Repositioned his bald spot, restacked his chins, glanced at his watch. "Shit." The meeting began in ten minutes. Hardly enough time to get ready. His antediluvian 'gänger was constantly under repair and he had been late four times this quarter. He couldn't remember which punishment a fifth offense merited: invective, Indian burn, or disembowelment...

He broke into a fastwalk, weaving and dodging the foot traffic of the slideways as he made his way towards the nearest launch pad. He tired out quickly and paused to catch his breath.

He was hungry. There was no time to be hungry.

Was there ever time for anything?

At the end of the block was a Bulimia Booth. He allowed the slideway to take him to it and ordered the day's special from a glowbot: synthetic imperial parrot deep-fried in human tears. The tears were fresh, cried by a group of orphans hanging upside down by their toes. The orphans were repeatedly spanked by a series of misshapen iron hands, and a consequential steady flow of tears leaked into the rusty fry basin beneath them.

By the time he arrived to the launch pad, Mr. Whackbottom had wolfed down the parrot, skeleton and all, and threw it up onto the Voltron hairdo of an endomorph. The hairdo exploded into separate pantherlike parts when the vomit struck it. Growling, the parts galloped down the stranger's arms, back and legs and disappeared into a sewer grate.

Mr. Whackbottom excused himself, handed the endomorph a blank check, and told him to buy a new hairdo. "Should you choose to buy more than a new hairdo," he added, "I shall summarily see to it that you and your immediate and extended family are swiftly infected by a Biblical plague. Good day, citizen."

Recognizing his face, the endomorph respectfully thanked the man and skulked away...

Mr. Whackbottom stepped onto the launch pad. He sucked in the overhang of his belly and pushed a button on his utility belt.

Goose bumps sprouted onto his flesh. The smell of absinthe ripped through his nasal passage...His body demolecularized into an iridescent, electric cloud of marbles. The cloud drifted into a flow-go, and 6.78 seconds later he stood on a plank outside a mirrored window, half a mile above the highest flyway in the district. Molarized now, he tightened the nub of his tie and tucked in his shirt as the window slid open and accommodated him.

In the upper tier of the Dumdum Tower, the tallest structure not only in Bliptown but in the entire Amerikan Midwest, were the offices, board rooms, meeting halls, sandwich shops, haberdasheries and whorehouses of the city's governing powers.

Five minutes ago, the congressman-things slipped on their respective nooses, kicked out the rocking chairs from beneath their feet, and hung themselves from the rafters of The Bronchial Theater. Ninety percent of the attendants were 'gängers. They dangled from the ceiling on interminable lengths of rope. Their thick, blubbery necks ensured that they wouldn't lose their breath, let alone crack their neckbones.

In the background, a technosubrealist rendition of German composer Edvard Grieg's creeping, rumbling Peer Gynt Suite No. 1, Fourth Movement, dimly played...and replayed...and replayed...

The congressman-things dangled in a broad circle and surrounded a small driftdisc. The driftdisc itself was surrounded by a red velvet curtain that, like the ropes, stretched twenty or so stories up to the ceiling.

The curtain opened 180 degrees and exposed Euclid Auchboom, 'gänger of Bartholomew Expletive, Speaker of the Theater, distinguished gentleman, and senior senior senior congressman-thing. It stared at the audience with wide white eyes, then tapped the side of its throat, producing a drawn-out metallic squink. The human congressmen-things wrinkled their noses.

"Here here," announced Euclid Auchboom. "This session of the Theater of the Perturbed will now come to order, the honorable Representative Gr. Euclid Auchboom, Representative of Representative Mr. Senior Senior Senior Distinguished Gentleman Congressman-Thing Bartholomew Expletive, presiding."

The blank-faced attendants lifted their right hands and snapped their fingers. They lowered their hands.

Gr. Auchboom nodded its obese head. "First on our agenda today is the matter of Representative Mr. Senior Senior Senior Distinguished Gentleman Congressman-thing Expletive's feelings. Since he took on a hermaphrodite as a mistress, he has been the butt of more than a few vulgar jokes. Not only does he feel badly when his colleagues make fun of him, he finds the act of joke-telling altogether distasteful. In his eyes, beings who tell jokes on a regular basis do so in an attempt to compensate for some flaw in their emotional disposition. They cannot bear the straight-faced drama of life and must attempt to animate it with humor. This is a weakness of character that also makes the revered, noteworthy and highly esteemed congressman-thing in question feel badly. I have been asked to tell you all that this unorthodox behavior will cease immediately. I won't name names, gentlemen, but the guilty parties know who they are." The 'gänger stared irritably at the guilty parties, one by one. "Questions?"

Silence except for the dry creak of swinging ropes...

"Fine. The matter is closed. Next on the agenda concerns the matter of my feelings. Specifically, I am referring to a nasty remark made about me by a congressman-thing who..."

As Gr. Auchboom continued, Mr. Horace Q. Whackbottom attempted to sneak into the theater. He deftly pushed open the giant, bronze Florentine doors of The Bronchial Theater's entrance and crawled in on his knees. He moved literally at a snail's pace for half a minute, grew impatient and picked up speed. His patience further diminished and he got to his feet and began to tip-toe towards his noose, slowly at first, then faster and faster, until he was dashing like an overweight ballerina across a stage.

All of the congressmen-things observed Mr. Whackbottom the moment he entered the doors. They continued to observe him with curious, mildly disgusted expressions as he attempted to be furtive. Even Gr. Auchboom, who was on the brink of tears because it suspected nobody took it seriously or wanted to be its friend, stopped speaking and fixed its gaze on the malefactor. Mr. Whackbottom didn't notice. His eyes were on the prize now, and he had blocked out the external world. Just a few more steps, he told himself, and I'll be hanging high and dry...

"Congressman-thing Whackbottom!" Gr. Auchboom shouted.

Freeze-frame…He glanced up at the assembly. Smiled. "Greetings, gentle colleagues. Apologies, apologies."

Mr. Whackbottom had been wrong about the punishment for this instance of tardiness. It was neither a tongue-lashing nor an Indian burn. Nor was it a mere disembowelment. It was all of these things at once.

At Gr. Auchboom's command, executioner androids sprung out of trap doors. Naked except for loose-fitting black felt masks with eye holes cut into them, they marched over to Mr. Whackbottom in fasttime and strung him up in his noose. One of the androids commenced hurling obscenities at him. Two others grabbed his forearms and squeezed and twisted them until they bled. The last one ripped off his shirt and gutted the congressman-thing with a discombobulator rod. The snakes and eels of his innards splashed onto the obsidian floor of the theater before he knew they had exited his body.

The Fourth Movement of Grieg's symphony reached its climax as Mr. Whackbottom screamed and struggled and kicked and screamed harder and louder…

He slumped over dead.

Trap doors engulfed the executioners where they stood. Two more trap doors spit out two more androids wearing florescent orange jumpsuits and carrying an array of janitorial equipment. They cleaned up the mess, disposed of Mr. Whackbottom's body, and likewise disappeared.

"Fine, fine," muttered Gr. Auchboom. "Note to self. Put an ad in the local tabloids for a new congressman-thing. Ad shall read: CONGRESSMAN-THING WANTED. NO EXPERIENCE NEEDED. COMPETITIVE SALARY. DOUBLE-CHIN REQUIRED, TRIPLE CHIN PREFERABLE. COMMUNICATION SKILLS PREFERABLE, BUT NOT REQUIRED. NO JOKE-TELLERS." The 'gänger dealt an admonitory glare to certain members of the audience. "15-25 HOURS PER WEEK. RESPONSIBILITES INCLUDE A TOLERABLE SENSE OF FASHION AND BEING ON TIME FOR CONGRESSIONAL MEETINGS. APPLICANTS SHOULD SUBMIT A WORD OF INTEREST NO LATER THAN

IMMEDIATELY. End ad." It took a deep, pensive breath. "All right then. Where was I? Ah yes. My feelings. You see, I am a delicate and sensitive flower..."

Gr. Auchboom explained just what kind of delicate and sensitive flower for twenty minutes before moving on to the next item, a concern for the lack of decent kitchenware on sale in Bliptown's ADWs. The android opened the floor for a formal discussion. There were a number of responses and calls to order. It was decided that three new brand names would be introduced into the market. Next were discussions on issues that included the poor selection of other household commodities, questionable trends in various subcommunal fashion statements, the overt introduction of two new professional sports (Tickleball and Beebopalulaball) into the city's socioeconomic curriculum by next year, and the covert introduction of two new belief systems (Sindieswitchism and Dentistology) into the city's religioeconomic curriculum by next month.

Then came the laws.

"I don't like Section 1,233 of Statute 46 of Law 20,035," blurted Congressman-thing Superspecificity when Gr. Auchboom opened up the floor. "I can't explain why, exactly. Lately I've just had a bad feeling about it. I had a dream about it the other night. I can't remember what happened in the dream, but it wasn't good. I move that we strike Section 1,233 of Statute 46 of Law 20,035 from the map."

Congressman-thing Midevolution's 'gänger perked up and its long feet began to wag. "I agree," it squawked. "I further Congressman-thing Superspecificity's proposal by suggesting that we pretend said section never existed in the first place."

Gr. Auchboom waited patiently for other interested congressman-things to chime in. Nobody did. It called for a vote. "Those in favor of Congressman-thing Superspecificity's proposal, say, 'Bring It On.'"

"Bring it on," droned a handful of congressmen-things.

"Those opposed, say, 'Horseshit.'"

"Horseshit," droned an equal number of congressmen-things in the same tone. The silent majority either didn't care, didn't like Congressmen-things Superspecificity and Midevolution, or were daydreaming.

"It's a tie!" Gr. Auchboom said excitedly. But why was it excited? It didn't even know what Section 1,233 of Statute 46 of Law 20,035 stipulated. And it disliked ties. Ties temporarily clogged the flow of congressional progress. If anything, the android should have been downtrodden. Perhaps there was a glitch in its negatronic brain, one that was beginning to pathologize its system-response mechanism. Perhaps it would soon be responding to everything put to it in precisely the *opposite* way in which everything put to it was supposed to be responded to. Perhaps it was already irrevocably schized. The thought worried Gr. Auchboom. For a moment, it experienced a profound sense of dread. But it quickly found its wits and, in a controlled voice, said, "Pardon me. The proposal shall therefore be deferred to a later, as-of-yet indeterminable date when Representative Mr. Senior Senior Senior Distinguished Gentleman Congressman-Thing Bartholomew Expletive is both present and sees fit to address it. Moving on, if you please."

For the next two hours, numerous laws and would-be laws were discussed in a similar fashion. Most of the discussions ended in ties with indefinitely deferred outcomes. Occasionally a vote resulted in a clear majority, at least in Gr. Auchboom's eyes, and a law was liquidated, revised, or conjured into existence.

The last thing under discussion concerned the holocausts being committed in Bliptown by the city's foremost mass murderers.

Gr. Auchboom hesitated to bring the matter up. The 'gänger cleared its throat uncomfortably. It fidgeted with its tie. "Lastly, I have been asked by Representative Mr. Senior Senior Senior Distinguished Gentleman Congressman-Thing Bartholomew Expletive, I repeat, by *Representative Mr. Senior Senior Senior Distinguished Gentleman Congressman-Thing Bartholomew Expletive*, to ask this committee its opinion on a rather controversial subject. Before I mention what this rather controversial subject is, I want to assure you all that I am under orders here. I have no desire to discuss it. I would prefer to not even think about it. I would prefer, in fact, to be alone right now, minding my own business and perhaps eating thinly cut slices of a ripe pear. I just want to make this perfectly clear before I proceed any further. Have I made this perfectly clear?"

A general rustle spread throughout congress.

Gr. Auchboom giggled nervously. "That's fine then. The subject I refer to is the recent string of holocausts that have been taking place within the perimeters of Bliptown's cityscape this morning. Specifically, the subject I refer to is that of a wayward plaquedemic and his psychotic 'gänger. As you know..."

It wasn't able to continue. The congressmen-things glanced at one another in horror and began to shout uncontrollably. Gr. Auchboom resisted the urge to break down and cry. It tried to appeal to its colleagues' good senses, but its voice was lost in the commotion, even when it maxed out its surroundsound volume control. The android quickly realized it would have to wait for congress to tire out. Standing tall and silent with chins upraised, it chewed on the inside of its cheeks and waited...

A minute and a half later, the Theater of the Perturbed was a spectacle of panting and wheezing as the congressmen-things, dangling there like winded cows, fought to catch their breaths. Those who had the means slipped their nooses onto a spare chin. A few almost cut themselves free of their nooses, but they refrained: to do so during a congressional session was heresy punishable by "soul removal," which entailed having one's heart skillfully ripped out by a Shaolin monk.

"Now that I have your attention again," Gr. Auchboom said, "I hope we can discuss this issue like gentlemen."

"Gentlemen?" carped Congressman-thing Yodelayheehoo, as if he had never heard the term before. "Isn't it illegal to even *speak* of such an issue? That's the Pigs' business! That's the Papanazis' business! That's the vigilantes' and the bounty hunters' business! That's everybody's business but ours!"

Gr. Auchboom's face puckered in consternation. "Grow up, Congressman-thing Yodelayheehoo."

"You grow up!" the man bleated, pointing his finger at the simulacrum-in-charge.

Other congressmen-things and 'gängers interjected. "I'm afraid to talk about the Dystopian Duo!" one of them exclaimed.

"Me too!" exclaimed another. "Punishment may result!"

Another exclaimed, "I don't like to be punished!"

Another exclaimed, "Punishment hurts me!"

Another exclaimed, "There's no place like home! There's no place like home!"

Another exclaimed, "This is illegal!"

Gr. Auchboom exclaimed, "It's not illegal if Expletive says it's not illegal!"

That quieted everybody down. Such an eminent congressman-thing's name wasn't often uttered without all of his titles, not to mention his first name. Gr. Auchboom motioned at the theater door. "If you gentlemen don't settle down, I'll be forced to seek out my superior. Is that what you want? He's busy right now, very busy indeed, but I'll interrupt him if I have to. I'll do it! Do you want me to do it?"

A man muttered. A 'gänger shook its head. A man and a 'gänger hung their heads and kicked out at the air like pouting little boys...

Gr. Auchboom nodded affirmatively, feeling extremely confident and powerful at the moment. It wondered how long the feeling would last. "Good! Now then. I want to reassure you that it pains me to address this subject as much as it pains you. But these two aberrations murdered a movie star in cold blood. I've only been asked to address the matter because of this sad fact. We can't just have private citizens running around killing movie stars. The social fabric would come undone. Killing plaquedemics, civilians, girl scouts, even Pigs is one thing. But a movie star? That's crossing the line, I'm afraid. Even though 'gängers do most of the acting for movie stars these days, their work is only validated by the public's knowledge of the existence of their original human figurations. In the absence of these figurations, 'gängers cease to have worth. That goes for 'gängers of all socioeconomic classes. There is no 'gänger more important than that which surrogates a celebrity. Thus Voss Winkenweirder's Victor Bleep, if it even recovers from the short circuit it experienced upon hearing of its original's death, will quickly be out of a job. Imagine what the Disunited Cities of Amerika would become if this kind of hoo-hah happened twice in one week! Things are bad enough right now. That's why an increasing number of celebrities are disappearing underground until the plaquedemic forest fire is put out. This is a trend that will no doubt continue. If these holocausts don't come to an end, two days from now the surface of the world could be entirely devoid of celebrities. That includes #1 Papanazi Hit Listers down to the most insignificant talk show hosts. The infrastructure of society is not in a position to support such a lack. Without celebrities, I suspect people's heads will begin to spontaneously combust on a mass scale. You know it's true, gentlemen. You understand the gravity of this situation, gentlemen. Now I ask you: what is Bliptown's Theater of the Perturbed prepared to do?"

A restless pause. Then:

"I don't feel good!" exclaimed a congressman-thing.

"Me either!" exclaimed a congressman-thing's 'gänger.

"I don't want to be a congressman-thing anymore!" exclaimed another congressman-thing.

And so on. As before, Gr. Auchboom waited for congress to tire out, threatened to tell Congressman-thing Expletive what was going on, and tried to reengage congress in a productive discussion. This happened four more times. Finally it was decided that the fate of Dr. ——— and Dr. Identity should be left up to everybody in the world save Bliptown's governing powers, but congress would make the following official statement to be printed in the Papanazi's foremost publications: "We the things of congress really, really encourage all Bliptownians to rise against and destroy the plaquedemic scourge that has beset our fine metropolis."

Gr. Auchboom struck a fist against its palm. "I hereby declare this session of the Theater of the Perturbed dismissed," it proclaimed. "Goodnight, gentlemen. Don't forget about the party at His Tragedy's estate this weekend. Mistresses only please. BYOB."

Grieg's symphony faded out as the members and surrogates of congress slipped out of their nooses and, massaging their necks and chins, filed out of the theater in an orderly line.

10
smaug turbo gt – 1st person (identity)

The Gumbo was inspired by the soup and morphed at my command. Sometimes it morphed of its own volition. One moment I looked like a movie star. The next I was a featureless nobody. Occasionally it actually took on the quality of gumbo soup. If I stuck out my tongue I could taste my head.

The Captain Crunch rendered my head something like a bear trap. It operated as a weapon as much as a fashion statement.

The Burroughs 5000 was a living ass that shat uncontrollably and uttered off-the-cuff hipster maxims in equal amounts. It also operated as a piece of weaponized fashion.

I had more conservative tastes and preferred the visages of historical figures. I tried on masks of Winston Churchill and Billy the Kid and Moses and Philip K. Dick and Siddhartra and Rapunzel and Malcolm X and Barry Manilow...I settled on Napoleon. I had no choice. They picked up the scent of our DNA...

The Law and their mythological hound dogs. The Papanazi. Fleets of vigilantes and bounty hunters...Dr. ———— said it looked as if we were towing a galactic cirque du soleil across town. He described the scene like a passage in a novel: "A glance in the rearview mirror showed the plaquedemics' carny skycraft and acrobats of all shapes, sizes and Technicolor costumes. It was a swarm of mad hatters, demonic trapeze artists, evil Elvis impersonators and unspeakable clowns. All of the alaristrians were technologized to the hilt. They jetpacked, rocketed, propellered and surfblazed after them alongside smartly insectlike turbogoblins, fangliders, Jackrippers, cloud cars, hangtanks, speedracers, Heinliners, hot air balloons and spitfire windmills, among other vessels. They shadowed the Dystopian Duo through a labyrinth of airways into the neoindustrial bowels of Bliptown with a balletic grace. There was no shaking the rabble off."

"Not bad," I said.

Dr. ———— clicked his tongue. "The end."

...I had just finished hotwiring a Smaug Turbo GT when the first group of Papanazis spotted us. The vehicle was an older but not outdated model of Acme's line of compact dragons. It was a two-seater with a small trunk and a barbed tail. Its long mouth contained spidersteel fangs and an oily tongue. Unfortunately it had been childproofed. Its fangs were corked. Its claws were manicured. And rather than fire it breathed Spaghetti-Os.

The engine of the Smaug was in its lungs. Its wiring was in its rectum. I stuck my fists into its anus and brought the beast to life...

The Papanazi opened fire on us.

The cockpit of the Smaug was in its plexiglass stomach. The flowfoam seats faced down but their backs were magnetically attracted to the spinal fluid of both humans and androids. We would have full movement of our limbs. But our backs would be fused to the machine.

I opened the cockpit. Dr. ———— and I huddled together and bent over. I commanded the Smaug to wake up and straddle us. The vehicle growled to sentience. It flapped its wings. It cracked its neck. Its iron knees crinkled and creaked as it stood up and positioned its open belly over us crooks.

Sparks ran down my lower vertebrae as we flew up into place.

"Ouch!" Dr. ———— shouted. He started to wheeze. "That stung. I think my back is broken."

I clamped my feet into place. "You're fine. Lock yourself in." I surveyed and fiddled with the controls. I tested the central joystick. I closed the hatch and told the Smaug to go. Papanazis circled us in a vicious frenzy.

The vehicle's barbed tail accidentally beheaded a Papanazi during liftoff.

Achtung Whoever-It-Was had been wearing a propeller beanie. The head twirled up and away and disappeared into a cloud of towerfog. The Papanazi's gesticulating body fell to the street.

I probably should have put the Smaug on autopilot. It could go faster and was more flexible and dynamic on its own. But I wanted to be in charge.

There was a retractable plug on the console. I shoved it into the cortical shunt behind my ear.

The Smaug's eyes and body and sensorium flooded into mine.

Two Papanazi landed on the underside of my neck during our ascent into the trafficways. They wore Stickem suits and crawled towards the cockpit to get clean footage.

I wriggled the skin of my neck until they fell off. I nailed them with a mouthful of Spaghetti-Os. A thousand cans of Chef Boyardee struck and stuck to their bodies and they pinwheeled away…

"My back hurts," Dr. ——— whined. "I'm getting hungry again. Food!"

"You're such a little girl. Be a man for once." I could communicate freely with my core body despite being jacked into the dragon.

"Be a man? Are you kidding me?"

"If I was kidding you I'd tell you so."

"No you wouldn't."

"That's true. At any rate, you don't have to be a man to be a man, 'Blah. You simply can't be afraid to serve the world a big silver platter of FUCK YOU now and then."

"FUCK YOU? What the hell is that supposed to mean?"

"You know what it means. It means reality. It means truth. It means humanity."

"That's the dumbest thing I've ever heard. What are you, a student-thing?"

"No. I'm Dr. Identity."

"What a stupid thing to say. What a lousy, stupid thing to say."

"You programmed me. You programmed me from A to Z. Hence it is retroactively you who says lousy, stupid things."

Dr. ———'s lips became a sphincter. "Don't call me 'Blah, goddamn it."

"Okay."

"I'm not kidding. I'm hungry."

"Check your pockets. You have enough food in your pockets to feed yourself until you die of old age. I don't understand it. You raided countless refrigerators at Littleoldladyville. Have you lost your short-term memory? Tell me what happened ten seconds ago. Do it."

"Don't tell me what to do."

"My pleasure. Do whatever you want."

He reached into a de la Footwa and pulled out a small bottle of milk and a box of Galaxian cereal. He opened the box. Little spaceships flew out in slowtime. He guppied them down. He took a swig of milk. "Ah," he said. He looked out of a porthole in the Smaug's underarm and blinked absently at the head-on collision of a cloud car and a flock of goosebikes. Screaming heads and flailing limbs squirted from the flames of the subsequent explosion.

Dr. ——— yawned.

The turbothrusters built into the Smaug's buttocks and calves kept us at a steady 80 mph. Its cumbersome wings were surprisingly resilient and acute. After a few bumpy warm-ups I was able to corner buildings and negotiate the narrow tunnels and pipelines and substreets of Bliptown with skill and precision.

The Law didn't waver. Nor did the Media and the Mad.

I slipped into oncoming traffic on Elemental Express. The vehicles and alaristrians that dodged and tumbled over my body effectively hindered our pursuers as they smashed into them. "An autopocalyptic lightning storm of kaleidoscopic gore lit up the sky behind the runaway plaquedemics," said Dr. ———...

I pulled ahead of the pack. I climbed and climbed and zigzagged through one grid of traffic after another. I penetrated the uppermost skyway and cut the power. I flapped in place and gazed down to see if anybody had stuck with me.

Just a few. Mostly Papanazi.

I drowned one in Spaghetti-Os. Another I impaled with the knifepoint of my tail. The last one I grabbed with my filed down claws.

A 'gänger. Stone-faced. Blinking at calculated intervals. Each blink preceded a powerful flash. I lifted the 'gänger to my eyes. Its pupils were silhouettes of pointing Uncle Sams.

I tightened my grip on the 'gänger. It continued to blink at me even as its bones fractured and splintered and it spurted designer blood. Finally its eyes burst and its head popped off. The blood surged out of its neck hole. I wondered if I could taste it through the matrix of the Smaug's tongue.

I took a lick.

It wasn't blood. It was wine. A medium-bodied Thunderlove Malbec produced eleven years ago according to my taste buds. Apparently the 'gänger operated as a wine receptacle and dispenser in addition to a vocational surrogate. Was it a fermenter and sommelier as well?

I drank the 'gänger dry. I burped. Pasta sauce swam up my throat. I coughed it out and discarded the empty body.

I told Dr. ——— that he ought to try that brand and year of Malbec.

"What are you, Dracula now?"

I reengaged the Smaug's engine and made for the summit of Bouffant Butte. "You programmed me as a wine specialist," I remarked. "Why is it you never filled my veins with wine? It's very fashionable."

"Fashionable my ass."

Bouffant Butte existed in an accelerated state of destruction and reproduction. I skirted scores of construction beams as I soared to the top of a tower entirely circumscribed by fire escapes. I realized the tower was nothing but fire escapes clumped and woven together and tied into great knots in places. Thousands of bodies scurried up and down the twisted iron stairways with no apparent purpose.

A bombardment of construction beams swung our way as I swooped around the building. I landed on a small platform on its opposite side and sat down. Our antagonists would probably find us without too much difficulty.

There was a chance they would pass us by. I didn't care one way or the other.

I jacked out of the Smaug.

Dr. ——— was having some sort of fit. He looked vaguely epileptic. "I remember my name!" he shrieked. "Identity, I remember my name!"

I cracked my neck. "Oh? I see."

"Do you?" The grin on his face seemed to want to wrap itself around his head. "It's Frank! Frank...Noble? Yes. Frank Noble. That's my name!"

"That's not your name." I shook my head. "That's not your name."

"Bull! I know what my name is!"

"Do you? What's your middle name? Do you have a middle name? And is Frank short for Franklin? Perhaps it's short for Frankfurter. Or Frankenstein. Or Frankly. Is your name Frankly?"

"That's funny. I'm serious."

I grabbed him by the shirt. "Look. You need to take it easy. Relax. Relax. Relax. Relax."

"Quit saying that!"

"Frank Noble is the name of a character in a novel. A novel you taught only last semester. Well, I taught it for you, but we talked about it beforehand in some depth. Remember?"

"I'm Frank. Frank*lin*. Let go of me."

I let go of him. "No. Frank*lin* Noble is a fiction. And an android. It single-handedly saved the planet Deleuzoguattari from destruction in the diegetic universe of the book *The Bald Conceptualization* from a post-post+postcolonial community of aliens who wanted to recolonize Deleuzoguattari and turn all of its flora and fauna back into its natural state of various outlandish cheeses. You empathized deeply with this character. Not only for would-be megalomaniacal reasons, but because you admired its system of values. You're simply projecting. You want to be in a position to save a world. Ironically, lately you've been demolishing a world. I have anyway. But that's more or less the same thing. The point is, Frank Noble is nothing but a combination of words that don't belong to you."

"Says you. We're not friends anymore. I want to go home. I miss my wife-thing."

"Your wife-thing?"

"Yeah!"

I calculated a response...and decided against it. "Why this obsession with your name? Who cares what your name is? You're defined by your actions and your technological extensions, not your signifier. Can't you just acclimatize to this piece of amnesia? The human inability to adapt never ceases to amaze me. There was a time when you were an adaptable species, you know."

"No, I didn't know that. I'm lucky you're here to tell me things. What would I do without you?'

"Be bored. Be disgruntled. Be lonely. Be desensitized. Be worthless. Be helpless. Be absurd. Be—"

"That'll do, Dr. Identity."

The Smaug sat on its backside with its legs hanging over the platform. We had a clear view out of the belly. The building across the way was a strip club erected in the form of a colossal naked lady. In silence we watched a team of construction workers scurry out of its high heels. A few seconds later there was an explosion. The building vaporized section by section from bottom to top. Almost immediately the construction workers returned and began to rebuild it in fasttime. Five minutes later they had already rebuilt the naked lady past its knees and halfway up its thighs.

We waited to see what would happen next.

11

dr. blah blah blah, a comic book – 1st person (identity)

"Did we lose them?"

"Shh."

I leaned my forehead against the glass of the Smaug's belly and peeked over its knees.

Two figures crept towards us on the exterior of a fire escape. I cracked open the Smaug's belly. I unscrewed one of my eyeballs and reeled it down towards them.

One was a bounty hunter. Like all of his kin he wore a campy polyester superhero costume with skintight leggings and tank top and glittery cape and shiny kneehigh boots and utility belt. Clenched between his teeth was a lawn mower blade.

The other figure was a professional vigilante's 'gänger. It also wore the apparel of its kind: stiff Toughskin jeans and a burlap sailor jacket and a Charles Bronson snowcap. Its hands had been surgically replaced with .457 magnums.

Neither of them saw my eyeball seeing them.

I flicked an incisor with the tip of my tongue. My eye retracted. I squished it back into its socket and took an exploding razorwire yo-yo out of my pocket. I opened the Smaug's belly further and leaned out. They were about ten feet below us.

I whistled.

Both figures glanced up at me. The bounty hunter was startled and the blade fell out of his mouth. It struck a railing and flipped behind him and plummeted...On its way down the sharp edge of the blade struck his heel just so and sliced it off. Blood gushed out of the heel hole in powerful spurts. The bounty hunter lost his footing.

Seconds later his cursing body surpassed the blade.

I raised an eyebrow to Dr. Blah Blah Blah. "That was easy." He ignored me.

The 'gänger shouted, "Hey! I see you up there!"

"I know you see me. I'm staring straight at you." I kicked the Smaug's belly all the way open and spun down the yo-yo...

On its first drop the yo-yo sliced off the 'gänger's ear. It removed an eyebrow and the tip of a nose and half a lip and a slice of chin on its second visit. Florescent green Inframan blood flowed out of its face. The 'gänger didn't flinch. I wondered what brand of pain receivers it had.

The yo-yo was on safety. I took it off safety and spun it down a third time.

The yo-yo rammed into the android's temple. It ticked. It tocked.

It exploded.

I slammed shut the Smaug's belly. Ersatz brains and chunks of skull splattered the glass.

I leaned back in my seat. "This is a piece of cake, Dr. 'Blah. Remarkable precision, these futuristic weapons. Don't you think?"

No response. No reaction at all. He stared into his lap and poked the insides of his cheeks with his tongue. Was he angry? Sad? Psychotic? Apathetic?

Did I care?

The Napoleon mask itched. I removed it and stretched on a syntheskin Abraham Lincoln mask complete with wart and bearded undercarriage and stovepipe top hat. "If I took my hat off I could probably pass for Henry David Thoreau. Don't you think so?"

Dr. 'Blah looked at me in disgust. "I don't think so. Thoreau was a goddamn hobbit. He was shorter than a male movie star. His head was half the size of Lincoln's. Be lucky if it was the size of Lincoln's fist."

"I'm not talking about size. I'm talking about physiognomy. Do I really have to point that out?"

"Anyway what was the story with those two assholes' beards? Where'd their mustaches go? What, were they Amish or something? They looked like fucking cartoon characters or something."

"They weren't Amish. As far as I know they weren't cartoons. They were Amerikans."

"Whatever. Did we lose them?"

"I don't know. I don't see anybody else out there right now. Give it another minute or two."

My original appeared to slip into a deeply meditative state. He broke out of it. "*Walden* sucks. The mass of men don't lead lives of quiet desperation. They lead lives of quixotic douchebaggery."

"Interesting." I glanced at Dr. 'Blah and smiled. "When all this is over, I think I'll write a memoir about our experience. Or a novel. Better yet, a comic book. Apropos I'll call it *Dr. Identity*. No, *Dr. Blah Blah Blah*. Unless you remember your real name, that is. The twist is that you'll be my plucky sidekick rather than the other way around. We'll live in a world where androids dominate and surrogate themselves with humans. I'll play the plaquedemic and you'll be my holocaustic 'gänger. Or maybe I'll make you a peaceful character. I'll make everything peaceful. We could live in a ridiculous utopia where everyone gets along and hugs each other. Instead of operating according to the Darwinist scheme of things, everyone will stink of altruism and good will. The setting will be pastoral—a jungle on Mars. We'll drink lemonade and eat apples and call each other 'sport.'"

Dr. 'Blah eyeballed me.

"Right. Hardly a marketable idea. Consumers pay for realism, not fantasy. It'll have to be a dystopia. And you'll have to be a homicidal maniac. More like the world we live in."

I tried to imagine the pictures that ran across Dr. 'Blah's mind's screen...

...and we were surrounded again.

And again they were mostly Papanazi. Some hovered in the air. Some clung to the Smaug's limbs. Some dangled from ropes out of hydracopters and hangtanks. They wielded every imaginable brand name of camera. We were drowned in heat lightning. I could feel it. For a moment I thought my beard had caught fire.

I took the Smaug off of standby.

I jacked in.

I pushed my body off the platform and tumbled into a gangly freefall. The Papanazi that clung to me lost their grips and shot into the sky. A few held on. I swatted or stabbed them with my tail until only one remained. He had crept onto the center of the Smaug's belly and wore a Stickem suit. Artificial spider legs jutted out of the suit's gooey flanks for auxiliary adhesiveness. His head was shaved and covered with thick-lipped jacks. The Papanazi blinked at Dr. 'Blah and me one at a time with illuminated blue eyes. Tattooed across his forehead was his name.

66.799

The Papanazi nodded politely at me. I nodded back.

Dr. 'Blah screamed.

I popped the childproof corks off my fangs with my tongue. I craned down my neck and took a vicious bite out of the Papanazi's back. By accident I tore out his spine.

The light in his eyes flickered out. His neck flopped back and his dead lips flapped in the whistling wind. His jacks wailed.

I spit out the spine and peeled the shell of Achtung 66.799 from my stomach as the ground sped up to meet us.

Dr. 'Blah screamed.

"I won't sell out entirely," I continued in a matter of fact tone. "I'm willing to cater to a mass readership in terms of *Dr. Bah Blah Blah*'s setting. Characterization and stylistics, however, are another issue. I refuse to develop my characters and make them round. My protagonists will be the epitome of flatness. You and I will lack histories. There will be no traumatic kernel of sociodesiring-production in our lives. We will exist on the surface of things. We will glide across the ice of the diegetic present without being able to dip down into the waters of history or leap into the sky of futurity. I will kill all metaphor and empower us by characterizing us as BwMs. It is only on the surface of the Body without Meaning, after all, that real issues like ultraviolence, perversion, and technosocioeconomic subjectivity can be addressed and explored. Also, character development takes too long. I don't have the patience for it, and I can't be bothered by it."

Dr. 'Blah screamed.

"Holster that drama."

I opened my wings. I energized my turbothrusters. I swam into the air in a stylish supersonic arch.

A pack of Papanazi suicide bombers had swandived off of the building after us without any means of propulsion. They snapped photos and recorded footage all the way down. I heard their bodies splat against the street as I swooped upwards.

Multiples of Papanazi stuck with us. And the Pigs and vigilantes and bounty hunters had caught up.

The chase was on.

I climbed into the sky. A building across the street imploded. I felt its impact in my sinuses and sneezed Spaghetti-Os.

Dr. 'Blah said, "Why couldn't you just let us crash! I'm sick of being alive! Enough already!"

"You don't want to die, Dr. 'Blah."

"Do I look like I'm enjoying being alive? Quit calling me 'Blah, damn you!"

A trough of Pigs jetted behind me and arbitrarily hacked at my legs with samurai swords. The scales of my skin consisted of a durable aluminopleather. The swords shattered when they struck it. But the Pigs just kept pulling more swords out of the trough. They seemed to have an endless supply.

I made a shishkebob out of them. I aligned myself with the trough and thrust my tail through their pink chests one after the other.

The trough fell out from beneath their speared bodies and smashed into a fangliding Papanazi. The fanglider snapped in two and caught on fire...

"Another thing. *Dr. Blah Blah Blah* will be told from multiple perspectives."

I dodged a volley of construction beams. I whiplashed the Pigs into a vidbuilding. "I'll employ various unreliable third-person narrators and diverse, perceptually inadequate first-person narrators. The primary reason for this aesthetic is flagrant: such a broken, scatterbrained multiperspectivalism will reflect the fragmented, schizophrenic, technosocioeconomic landscape of the comic's diegetic reality. Under this auspice, I have the freedom to be atemporal and alinear at will and nobody can hold me accountable for not piecing together a coherent, edge-of-your-seat, empathic, hyperformulaic story. Monoperspectival stories with beginnings, middles and ends are a one-way ticket to Ennuiville. That's what the 1% of the consumer public who still reads wants, of course, but I won't cater to that excremental demographic. I'll create something pure and new. *Dr. Blah Blah Blah* will be an original production."

I began to spit Spaghetti-Os over my shoulders at random intervals. Most of the pursuers I hit fell. A few 'gängers ate their way through the artillery.

"You can't create something new," said Dr. 'Blah. "The new is just the old in disguise. Making something new is merely the process of disguising something old in a seemingly creative way. The disguise is the thing—not the thing itself. You're living proof of this, Dr. Identity. You are the 'new' disguise of the me-thing. All 'gängers are." He folded his arms across his chest triumphantly.

"That's an insightful point. Well spoken indeed."

"Fuck you."

"Even more insightful."

I dizzied our antagonists by circling a vidbuilding in a highspeed candystripe path. "Who will be my narrators?" I said rhetorically. "What will be the ratio of human to android narrators? What will this ratio suggest about the universe of my text? How will I represent the thinking of a machine? You and I exhibit similarities in our cognitive praxes, for instance, but there are marked differences, namely in that the meat of my psyche is constituted by digits, numbers and equations whereas yours is constituted mainly by media images. But this is my comic book world. Cognition doesn't need to be a narrative factor. I could care less about cognition anyway. What matters is how one extends oneself, not how one conceives of extending oneself. Action, reaction—not clockwork. The only narrative factors I care about are description and dialogue. Everything else is bird shit. Plot especially. Plot is for plaquedemics. So is exposition. There will be no outright exposition. Any insight into the machinery of my diegesis and its characters will have to be extracted from the context of the comic's descriptive momentum, which will be conducted by visual imagery. Luckily my program consists of drawing and illustrating skills. These skills are limited to just a few out-of-vogue styles, but if I mix and match them in the proper way, I suspect I can devise a cartoonesque aesthetic that at least approaches my current vision of *Dr. Blah Blah Blah*. You know what Benjamin says: 'The work of art is the death mask of its conception.' But I have a feeling my death mask will surprise you. I dare say it will transcend the acuity and *savoir faire* of its conception. Hold on."

We reached the top of the vidbuilding. I landed on the edge. I turned around sharply and karate chopped a bounty hunter. The lightweight fabric of its superhero suit and the texture of my skin wasn't a good combination for him. My aluminopleather claw passed through his babysoft flesh and sliced him in two. His screaming torso tumbled into the spinning tentacles of a hydracopter and shredded...Blood and entrails splattered the hydracopter's windshield. The vehicle swerved out of control...

Cameras popped and flashed and focused and clicked and blipped and winked and blinked and blasted and machinegunned and fluttered and fizzed and smoked and snapped and exploded...I jumped off of the vidbuilding. I fell into a daredevil dive. I planed out and set a course back towards the heart of Bliptown. Bouffant Butte faded into the distance behind the teeming swarm of mediatized warriors.

Dr. 'Blah had grown silent. He wasn't moving. His face wasn't even twitching. His eyes were empty. I asked him if he was all right. He made a sound that resembled the greeting of a sick duck.

I said, "Not to worry, Dr. 'Blah. *Dr. Blah Blah Blah* will be a great success. I can see the entire project unfolding into the horizon of my mind's screen. I suspect the completed work will garner a Bliptown Book Award. Perhaps it will even receive the illustrious Stick Figure Prize. What a treat that would be." The Stick Figure Prize was the most widely respected and desirable commendation in technoliterature named after a man who was born an actual stick figure with twiglike legs and arms and a nearly featureless bowling ball for a head that sat atop his pencil-neck. His body was jet black and seemingly two-dimensional. They named the prize after him not because he was a literary auteur or benefactor but because technically he wasn't supposed to exist. In other words he was a living fiction. "I know you've had aspirations of receiving the Stick Figure Prize for your own work. Maybe if you finish the comic book you've been writing for the past ten years? No hard feelings if I happen to receive it. I know you'll be supportive. Why wouldn't you be supportive? I'm your 'gänger. My accomplishments are a direct reflection of your character."

"Quack," said Dr. 'Blah.

I liquidated a handful of Papanazi. "Speaking of your character, I think I'll represent you as a drag queen. I must admit I've discerned certain transsexual tendencies in your mentality and behavior since the day you purchased me. The question, then, is what sort of dresses will I put you in? I have a masculinized fashion sense and I'm not altogether keen on feminine apparel. Here is the research element of the project."

"Quack," said Dr. Blah.

"And so your character's penchant for ultraviolence will stem from a preposterous, unspoken insecurity regarding sexuality. An atrocious cliché, I know it. But I can't help wondering—"

An explosion rattled my sensorium. I was soaring down Grape Ape Alley at a speed approaching 100 mph and began to slow down. At first I didn't realize what had happened.

Then I felt the flames. My wings were on fire and a smoking hole beleaguered my back.

I flapped and fanned my wings on the flames in hopes of putting them out. They spread.

I jacked out of the Smaug and took the controls. "We're going down." The vehicle plunged into the whirling city.

Dr. 'Blah regained the power of speech. "It's about time!"

The wind whistled. Outside the belly of the Smaug the world was fireworks and gore and electricity and burning flesh...

I judiciously rearranged my top hat. I stroked my beard. I gripped the lapels of my shirt. "If destruction be our lot, we must ourselves be its author and finisher..."

12
cronenberg cirque – 3rd person

Achtung 66.799's jacks tried to pick another fight. They covered his skull like moon craters and ran the length of his scoliotic spine. His body vibrated in the torrent of their harangue.

The jacks barked at a meteorologist in Biospeak. The meteorologist, Bario Ackalacka, worked for Channel 10,443. This morning his bright-eyed 'gänger informed the Papanazi that the local government had conjured and dispersed an übertsunami that was scheduled to sweep through his neighborhood this afternoon and give it a moral cleansing, countering and quashing the wave of crime that had recently crashed there. Ackalacka was a tall, bronze, ripped up body engineer with a purple face that looked like a fist. He had on a thong and cowboy boots with spurs. An exoskeleton of veins encrusted his skin. Achtung 66.799 wondered if the meteorologist could understand Biospeak. He hoped not. He wasn't armed. Not with muscle, not with hardware. Not even with Biospeak.

Served him right. He had bought the jacks from a street surgeon recommended by an underground talk show host. At first he was only going to have one jack installed. But they were dirt cheap and he decided to load up. Achtung 66.799's identity demanded a multiplicity. So did his fashion sense. The street surgeon assured him they were no-nonsense implants. User-friendly and fully functional. But after installation the metallic rings that described their exteriors morphed into fleshy grey lips and their pistils became lizardlike tongues. They were sentient, too. Achtung 66.799 wondered if the surgeon had sold them to him because he didn't like his looks, he wanted to play a joke on him, or he couldn't get the things off of his hands. Probably all of the above.

He knew a few words of Biospeak, mostly obscenities, so he understood some of the hash his jacks slung out. Ackalacka didn't seem to notice. He continued to sip his drink and slap the ass cheek of the android standing next to him at the bar. The music was the usual vintage cacophony of synthesizers, riffblitzes and metronomics, but it wasn't turned up that loud. The meteorologist probably didn't speak the language.

Achtung 66.799 tried to ignore his technology.

Failed.

He tried to reason with his technology.

Failed.

He tried poking and prodding his technology with a drink stirrer. That worked a little. His jacks' hullabaloo grew louder and people started giving him dirty looks. But at least the hullabaloo was directed towards him now.

At one corner of the bar, a Guy Smiley impersonator spooned rabbit pellet pasta, Cronenberg Cirque's specialty dish, into an oversized ersatz grin. Sidling up next to him, Achtung 66.799 stole a noodle from the Smiley's plate. He found a dark corner and used the noodle to methodically beat his jacks into submission. Initially they got mad, threatening to turn inside out and eat him. Then they got tired and fell asleep. A series of soft, electric snores escaped the Papanazi's body...

He had been following the plaquedemics when they ducked into Cronenberg Cirque. He had been following them all day, in fact, but still hadn't retained a money shot. The ideal money shot would capture them red-handed in an *au naturel* moment, free of all masks and costumes. This was unlikely considering the plaquedemics' egregious penchant for Halloweenlike behavior. He could still land a decent fee, however, for a clip of them in disguise, depending upon how he contextualized his report on the footage when he wrote it up. So far he couldn't even manage to get footage of them in any form.

No sign of the plaquedemics now. He suspected they had retired to a psychostall and jacked into the Schizoverse. Cronenberg Cirque's psychostalls were first rate—a wide selection of wireless enterological instruments and almost no static on the Idside.

One wore a white three-piece suit and beret and his face was a dark block of blunt edges. The other was decked out like a flapper—bobbed hair, dumb-looking smile, dress like a purple weeping willow tree, fishnet tights and high-heel clogs. Achtung 66.799 wondered if they were aiming for a Great Gatsby vogue; the male looked like Robert Redford in the 1974 film. He remembered the film from his brief stint in college. He remembered the novel, too. It was the only novel he read before getting expelled for running away from a plaquedemic who tried to cut his head off for answering a question incorrectly. Then again, maybe they were just voguing the Roaring 20s. A Roaring 20s fashion craze had materialized yesterday afternoon. It was outdated now, but as always plenty of hangers-on refused to make the change to the craze of the moment, which, as far as Achtung 66.799 could tell, seemed to be a combination of Bohochic, Discofever and Diagnostic Zero. Still, the Dystopian Duo fit in just fine.

Why they changed their outfits so often didn't make sense to Achtung 66.799. They were like a couple of kids playing dress up. As a result, the Papanazi almost lost them a few times—especially when they ducked into phone booths or revolving doors on crowded streets, changed outfits in fasttime, and emerged in various Golden Age superhero disguises that allowed them to blend in with the odd flock of bounty hunters that prowled the streets, slideways and flyways. On one occasion they came out of a phone booth as animé versions of Batman and Robin. Their cartoon eyes were the same—two glossy, long-lashed orbs that appeared to be on the brink of shedding tears—and he couldn't tell which was which. Clearly the plaquedemic playing Robin had had better days. His neon green briefs were too small and his testicles kept popping into view. Achtung 66.799 struggled to get a clean shot of him, but there were too many bodies, and a moment later they had each turned into somebody else...

In addition to their ever-changing identities, the plaquedemics were difficult to track because they moved so quickly from place to place, perpetrating one holocaust after another. But the Law wasn't the only doghouse that could sniff out DNA. Achtung 66.799 had his own sniffer. It wasn't very fashionable. It was no more than a large rubber nose connected to a pair of plastic thick-rimmed spectacles and a fake bushy mustache. Hardly a DNA hound. But it did the job.

Cronenberg Cirque had two hallways of psychostalls: business class, economy class.

Achtung 66.799 slunk into the latter.

A Hal 9000 eye embedded in the wall stopped him. "Excuse me," it said blankly. "Payment please."

"Oops. Sorry." Achtung 66.799 leaned over so that he was eye to eye with the HAL. The HAL scanned his retinal databank and extracted payment.

"I can feel it." It burped. "Have a nice day."

Buzzing blacklights hanging from the ceiling by long, macrobiotic tendrils swung back and forth. The air smacked of moth balls. Achtung 66.799 proceeded down the hallway, hurriedly peeling back velvet curtains, peering into this psychostall, that psychostall, and inhaling, inhaling, inhaling...Time was his enemy. No telling what the plaquedemics might look like when they left the place, or from what direction they might leave the place, or what sort of ultraviolence they might enact as they were leaving the place. Also, a Schizoversal clip of them would be priceless, no matter what form they took on the Idside. He could tangibly retire from the Papanazi. Assuming that they were even jacked in.

They were. He smelled them. Suddenly their scent was so powerful he felt nauseous.

He disappeared behind a curtain.

Standing before him like two deactivated sentinels were the naked Egos of Dr. Identity and Dr. ———. The Egos were unidentifiable. As with all residual bodies, they existed as faceless, holographic, anthropomorphic bundles of nerves. No denying the stench of their DNA, though. Achtung 66.799 smiled and removed his nose.

Despite how many times he had been in the presence of barenaked Egos, the sight unsettled him. When the Schizoverse confiscated your Id, it confiscated your body, the flesh being indivisible from Desire and Instinct. Left behind was a virtual incantation of the Ego, that psychic hard-on General Freud believed to be the mediator between the passionate, irrational Id and the guilt-ridden Superego as well as the conscious sense of the self and that which allowed the Id to negotiate reality. Triangulated in this way, the Ego figured as a dynamic "personality." Separated from this triangulation, however, it was a soft jelly thing, a deserted, lackluster shell with nothing to do but listen to the whiny inner voice of its Superego complain about the social, moral, ideological, metaphysical and ontological terminal choices of its defiant Id.

Jacking into the Schizoverse was not unlike being stuffed into a de la Footwa pocket. Achtung 66.799 knew this because he had suffered from the experience as a child.

The memory still harrowed him. He was in the third grade. Don Jacoby Kish, mob boss of Tweedle Dee Elementary School, had fingered him for a hit because he didn't like the way he chewed his food. "He chews too slow," Don Kish informed his joeboys, "and he pushes his lips out too far. Deal with the turd."

Don Kish was one of only three children attending Tweedle Dee who owned pants sporting de la Footwa pockets. At the time the pockets were relatively new on the market. His father's 'gänger's 'gänger had rubbed out a rival family's boss's 'gänger's 'gänger's 'gänger and seized the pants as booty. (In many communities, even surrogates necessitated surrogates.) The joeboys nodded and waited for their boss to remove his pants. They were tight on his chubby little legs and it took a while for him to grunt and squirm out of them. The joeboys pretended like Don Kish's struggle with the garment was perfectly natural, staring at their toes with their sharp dunce caps tilted just so…

Recess lasted from nine to five at Tweedle Dee except for two fifteen minute class sessions in the morning and afternoon and a two hour midday break for lunch. As such, the protoplaquedemic faculty who worked at the school had sufficient time to conduct orgies without being bothered by the tedium of elementary education. Achtung 66.799 had just finished eating lunch. A hall monitor who refused to let him stay inside and study his times tables dropkicked him back out onto the playground. Friendless, he retired to a remote spot on the playground and recommenced burying boogers in the dirt. A mischievous protoplaquedemic once told him the boogers would grow into muscular scarecrows. He was planting a whole field of them in hopes that, someday, there would be enough scarecrows to play Duck-Duck-Goose with as well as to beat up anybody that fucked with him.

He got worked over by three of Don Kish's joeboys. They interrupted Achtung 66.799 as he lowered a booger into a hole by a fish hook, whispering encouragement to it. "You can do it. I believe in you. You have the power." They crept up behind him and punched and kicked and picked him up. One of the joeboys had put on the don's pants. The pants hung on his legs like two sewn together laundry bags and had to be held onto his waist by another joeboy while the third joeboy did the dirty work. Achtung 66.799 shrieked for help. The two playground supervisors on duty heard him, but they were 69ing in a treehouse and couldn't be bothered. The joeboys flipped him over and his head deterritorialized into infinite molecules of raw, red consciousness...

The pain was inexplicable. But it only lasted a moment.

Achtung 66.799's body reterritorialized inside of the de la Footwa in a much smaller, slightly altered form. Only 100,000th his actual size now, he was a featureless homunculus floating in a sea of hyperamniotic fluid. His arms and legs didn't work. He couldn't taste or smell or feel. He could barely see...aggressive mothman shadows...flickering stars and nebulae...random body parts and human bones...scores of Fisher Price weapons...thousands of Hostess products...

He cried.

He couldn't cry.

He went insane.

He didn't know how long he spent in the pocket. He figured he would die there.

Then he was lying at the feet of Don Kish, hacking up algae and mud.

"That'll teach ya to chew your food like an asshole," said the don, and urinated on him. The joeboys did the same.

Achtung 66.799 exited the boy's room that was Don Kish's office and stumbled down the hallway. Nobody in sight.

"Mom!"

Hot yellow urine trickled down his arms, soaked through his clothes, dribbled from his ear lobes. One droplet seeped onto his eyeball. It felt like a bee sting. He clawed and scratched at his eye and tried to tear it out. He ran up and down the hallway, screaming, cursing...Nobody heard him. Nobody saw him.

He decided to go to the gymnasium and hang himself from the basketball rim. He knew about hanging because his grandfather was a politician. Unlike his grandfather, however, he had a perfectly breakable neck...

Inside of the gymnasium a teeming mound of protoplaquedemics conducted a great S&M orgy. The mound more or less encompassed the entire basketball court and rose halfway to the ceiling. Whips, chains and genitals flailed from its spurting, gelatinous body like the tentacles of electrified octopi.

"Mother?" said Achtung 66.799.

The assistant principle of Tweedle Dee, Mr. Beanfiend, was near the top of the mound and saw the boy come in. He holstered his penis, loosened his dog collar, slicked back his Mohawk, placed a megaphone to his lips and shouted, "Security!"

The Pigs fell on Achtung 66.799 instantly...

Shortly after the incident, Achtung 66.799 established the Community of People Who Are Interested in Eating Their Own Arms (CPWAIETOA). The idea was that if only a small piece of one's arm were eaten at a time, a piece no bigger than a hangnail, then eventually the whole arm might be consumed with a minimal amount of pain and virtually no bleeding. He didn't have many takers. As it turned out, he only had one taker aside from himself, a girl named Spinrad Gizzard born with a birth defect called phocomelia who didn't have any arms to begin with: two long, boneless hands dangled limply from her shoulders. Achtung 66.799 himself only made it a tenth or so of the way down one of his pinky fingernails before abandoning the cause. In retrospect, he realized his misrepresented desire to found CPWAIETOA stemmed from the mental trauma inflicted on him by Tweedle Dee's protoplaquedemics and ruling mob boss.

Achtung 66.799 generally experienced happy days in the Schizoverse. But jacking in always reminded him of the time Don Kish sentenced him to a de la Footwa. The proximity of a plug, in fact, elicited feelings of anxiety and dread. As he stood before the Egos of Dr. Identity and Dr. ——— and regarded the wide variety of enterological plugs hanging on the corkboard behind them, vertigo swept over him and he nearly lost control of his bladder...

He shook it off. Bliptown was barely functional in the wake of Voss Winkenweirder's death, and he needed footage of the movie star's killers for his own financial well-being as much as for the emotional well-being of a general public who wouldn't be satisfied until they gorged themselves on a sufficiently overwhelming feast of media imagery featuring the plaquedemics and their antics. Achtung 66.799 transformed into soldier mode. He closed his eyes, took a deep breath, and flexed the flaccid cords and wires in his body that were supposed to be muscles.

Beneath the corkboard was a console. Achtung 66.799 could use it to track the plaquedemics' position in the Schizoverse. He began to fiddle with the controls...and one of his jacks woke up. It emitted an obnoxious yawn and complained about a nightmare and persistent halitosis. Its bitching woke up the rest of the jacks, who also began bitching about bad dreams and bad breath.

Achtung 66.799 pinpointed his mark and then surveyed the designer plugs that would deliver him into the Schizoverse. They came in all brands and fetishes, ranging from ordinary kitchen knives to hacked off human fingers to petrified eels to a slue of biological dildos.

"One of you is in for a treat," smiled the Papanazi. The jacks keyed up. All at once they screamed, "Me! Me! Me!"

The jacks on his skull were the most efficient, supplying the cleanest Idside experience, whereas the ones on his back were mostly for show.

Achtung 66.799 told the jacks that, to be fair, he would eenie-meeni-mini-moe a winner. "That's the kind of gentleman I am," he said, hoping they would appreciate the gesture.

They didn't. They accused him of being a pussy and lacking the balls to take charge of situations by means of his own conscious volition. Then they began attacking the character of his penis. Achtung 66.799 reminded them they lacked eyes and had never seen his penis or interacted with it in any way for that matter. They told him they knew all about his penis based upon his personality, which was fraught with deep-seated insecurities. They continued to emasculate him until Achtung 66.799 gave up trying to reason with them and selected a course of entry.

The Razortickler was a living, breathing organism that emitted an orgasmic sigh when he clenched its handle. It cried out in ecstasy somewhere inside of his head when he rammed it into the loudmouth above his right temple. Blood splashed out of the jack as the microblades took their toll.

An aura of static electricity formed around Achtung 66.799's body. Then his flesh, bone and Inner Beast slurped up, up and away...

His Ego hung its metaphorical head as the voice of his Superego reaffirmed what the jacks had told him about his manhood.

13
schizoverse, part 1 – 3rd person

They looked distinctly computer-generated yet purely organic. Their ragtime fedora hats were as acutely defined as their black-and-white physiognomies and the blades of the hypersharp hardware clenched in their mitts.

One of them smiled an upside-down smile. The other nodded and leapt twenty feet in the air. He slipped into slowtime on his ascent, trenchcoat fluttering...When he reached his peak, a rhizome of lightning flashed overhead, illuminating a boundless skyscape of ultraviolence. Infinite Ids and feminIds of all figurations clashed and inflicted the maximum degree of damage. A steady downpour of blood, viscera and body parts rained from the skyscape. Most of the carnage caught fire and vaporized before it struck the ground as terminated players were evicted back to their realtime selfhoods. Nonetheless if you were scrimmaging on the battlefield of the Schizoverse, the iconography of your body was invariably soaked in hot, sizzling gore...

The warrior slipped into fasttime on his descent. His opponent countered the maneuver and gauged a striking distance...He spun out of the way. His attacker came down on the spot of ground that was supposed to be his opponent's head. His knees locked and exploded like sticks of dynamite. Thin jet streams of saliva rode the wave of the scream that ushered out of his round, white mouth...

The calves, ankles and feet of the kneeless warrior crumbled to neon ashes beneath him. He fell onto the gaping, bleeding stumps of his legs. Another wet scream. The body teetered and swayed...then tilted forward...His beaklike nose slammed into the terracotta street.

His opponent dodged a severed head the size of a Japanese football that had been catapulted at him. Fights the likes of this one spanned the length and breadth of SS (Schizo Street) Bongodome. Every warrior was in constant danger of fallout from every direction.

He triumphantly approached his victim...Impossible slime and gristle gushed out of the stumps, and a moat of mud boiled around his head as he struggled to wrench his nose free...A boot stomped on the back of his head, burying it underground...Extremities flailed in the bloodshower...Trenchcoats fluttered, eyes blazed white...A glistening glowsword brandished, set against the scintillating night...

He sliced the body in two. Its lower half helicoptered away while its torso remained planted upside-down in the ground. Viscera poured out of the fresh wound with renewed vigor.

It was at this moment that Achtung 66.799 made the scene.

Crouched in a fetal position, the naked Id cooed and sucked his thumb. He quickly shook off this piece of return-to-the-wombitis, however, and stood up. Squirming black entrails singed from his gray skin. His jacks were gone, confined to the matrix of the real world...

The Papanazi darted across the street towards the saloon. His hyperbolic, overinflated penis led the way.

The triumphant Id had set his sights on him now. He charged, swinging the glowsword from hip to hip in fasttime.

Achtung 66.799 couldn't allow himself to be killed. There were times when it had taken him days to colonize a stillzone of the Schizoverse. He would jack in and immediately be offed and his flesh would be thrown back out into the real world. Then he would be denied access to that particular region of the Schizoverse for a 24 hour period—a universal punishment for being terminated there. If terminated now, he would have to jack into a different, adjacent region and make his way back to this one, a trek that would certainly see him pseudomurdered again along the way. By then the plaquedemics would be gone, jacked out or relocated.

The great burden of Achtung 66.799's elephantine genitals was a common, natural condition in nearly every male and shemale who jacked in. It necessitated that battlefielders strapped the genitals to their legs or looped and tied them around their waists. This of course became problematic when the thrill of combat and ultraviolence incited a sexual reaction and one's penis stiffened without warning. But the Papanazi was already stiff, his Id-body still adjusting to the eroticized diegesis of the Schizoverse. Even if he wasn't stiff, he had no time to stow away the terminal extremity. He hugged it against his chest as he plodded towards the entrance of the saloon.

Two steps from a little stairway that led up to overtall swinging doors, his antagonist dealt him a flying kick to the kidney. The Papanazi somersaulted forward, twice, and landed on his epic penis. The wind was knocked out of him and he couldn't breath.

He turned his head and glanced over his shoulder. He wanted to see what was coming. Death meant nothing in the Schizoverse. An Id could die again and again in any number of creative, tortuous, and obscene ways and come back for more as often as he, she or it pleased. The only way out of the Schizoverse was death, in fact. Unfortunately death hurt. The Schizoverse was a psychological fiction. But the pain one experienced Idside of that fiction was very real. For some reason, pain and death didn't hurt Achtung 66.799 quite as much if he were in a position to watch how somebody inflicted it on him.

The skyscape exploded with lightning again. Looming over the Papanazi, the Id was shadowcast except for his brilliant grin and eyes. His flared, flapping trenchcoat resembled a cape, and he looked vaguely like a cartoon. His image belonged in a comic book, Achtung 66.799 thought, remembering, as if for the first time, that the entire Schizoverse was a comic book world, a video game, basically, with exceptional graphics and a perverted realization of the potentials of digitized flesh.

He tried to beg for his Id's life. An inarticulate wheeze came out. The shadow of his antagonist's head nodded, his grin disappeared, he flaunted his weapon...

The weapon toppled out of his grasp as his opposing arm was ripped out of its socket by a feminId in an arachnosuit with iron fangs. Blood sprayed out of the wound in a potpourri of neon red sparks. The feminId ate half of the arm in two gruesome bites and spit the remainder out. Then she leapt onto the Id and squeezed the Technicolor juices out of him with razorwire legs. Both creatures emitted uniquely horrific cries.

Achtung 66.799 crawled up the stairs, across the porch and into the saloon...

"Safe!" hooted an Id as the Papanazi entered the swinging doors. Appropriately, the Id had on an umpire uniform with spiked shoulder pads and a mask that was a baby kangaroo's ribcage. He made a gracefully overindulgent cutting motion with his arms and asked, "May I interest the new mister in a fashion and/or weapon statement, cutting edge or otherwise?"

"Please," Achtung 66.799 panted.

He followed the umpire's lead into a coffin, his erection dipping to half mast. Some Ids and feminIds preferred nakedness in the Schizoverse, namely the orgiastics, which comprised roughly thirty-five percent of the population of the Schizoverse at any given time, a healthy compliment to the majority populace of battlefielders. The Papanazi preferred the comfort and reassurance of vogue. Even when time didn't permit it. Right now his mind was set on a very specific vogue.

The coffin stood on end in a dusty, cobwebbed corner. Its door opened. A creaky, metallic voice invited Achtung 66.799 inside. The door shut behind him. The voice asked if he was having a good day.

"What's a good day?"

The coffin's glimmering, pulsing walls geometrically unfolded...bifurcated... multiplied...morphed...in fasttime, in fasttime...Ten seconds later he stood on a driftdisc in the middle of a virtual ADW. Surrounding him was a labyrinth of shelves and racks containing the most elite, middle- and low-class clothing and artillery available on the market. Most of the clothing consisted of new-and-improved brands of trenchcoats and fedoras—the Schizoverse's signature articles of fashion—and the artillery consisted mainly of technetronic blades, swords, throwing stars, chainsaws and other slice-and-dice objects. Guns, while not illegal, were far less effective media for inflicting the highest extreme of ultraviolence and eliciting the most pain and gore from the human body.

Achtung 66.799's mind automatically linked to the driftdisc. He told the mechanism what he wanted and it guided him across a quarter mile of empty green space to a set of hangers and shelves containing the day-to-day visages of any number of plaquedemics. He sifted through them and selected one. Far too expensive. But home base would comp him if he landed a money shot, and given his near miss with pseudodeath a minute ago, he was in a gambling mood. He stared at the barcode on the product long enough for it to read and rob his retinal databank. Then he stared at the barcode on a vintage ray gun. Bad form, no doubt, but he might need the protection. And at some point he would need a way back into the real world. He preferred suicide to being butchered by a stranger.

The ADW collapsed and the walls of the coffin reformed around the driftdisc as quickly as they had blown apart.

The coffin door opened.

Out walked the figuration of Humidor Tang, twenty-second century speculative fiction writer and distant relative of the inventor of Tang orange-flavored drink crystals, Charles Mayfield Tang a.k.a. William "Doll Hair Bill" Mitchell. The Papanazi had done a little research on Dr. ——— and learned that he held Humidor Tang in high literary esteem; he hoped dressing like the writer would allow him to get close to the plaquedemic, if not befriend him.

Tang looked the role. He had a slight hunchback, a dandruff-strewn whirligig hairdo, a lopsided beer belly, a fixed I-have-low-self-esteem facial expression, a tiny v-beard beneath his underlip, surgically altered Vulcan ears, and no sense of fashion whatsoever—all symptoms of the proverbial speculative fiction writer. The synthetic facemask felt heavy on Achtung 66.799's cheeks and neck. He adjusted to it quickly. He never adjusted to his outfit—worn black clogs, skintight burlap bellbottoms, flashy wildwest belt buckle, moth-eaten T-shirt, flannel overshirt with too-short sleeves—but that was inevitable in

131

terms of appearance. In terms of comfort, he hoped that the outfit's prosthetic stomach would offset and balance out its prosthetic hunch. It didn't. Both attachments seemed to want to tug him in different directions. When he walked, it looked like he was being punched gently in the shoulderblade and the bellybutton, one at a time.

Achtung 66.799 finger-saluted the umpire as he turned the corner. He lumbered through another set of swinging doors and entered the main room of the saloon. Behind him the umpire called another Id safe.

Crowded here. Shoulder-to-shoulder in some areas. Genital-to-genital in others. Powerful, high-paced banjo Melodrome ripped through the joint like a tornado, occasionally knocking bodies off of their feet. The Schizoverse was a playspace and most of the saloon's occupants were human save the odd 'gänger. In the past androids couldn't lawfully enter the Schizoverse. At one point it was collectively referred to as the Last Human Frontier. Eventually people became disinterested in recreation, however, and started to send their 'gängers in to play for them.

Ironically 'gängers' Ids and feminIds looked perfectly human except for their big white eyes. Human Ids and feminIds, on the other hand, retained the shadow of their basic appearance, but they looked more like stock EBEs with hairless gray skin, thin limbs, sharp black eyes, pointy chins, and bald bulbous heads. This assumed one wasn't in costume. Most costumes were incredibly lifelike and ranged from giant insects and vermin to cartoon characters to mythical beasts to talk show hosts and movie stars. Achtung 66.799 noticed a surplus of Voss Winkenweirder lookalikes. He knew Dr. ——— and Dr. Identity would be disguised. He just hoped they weren't disguised beyond recognition.

He spotted the plaquedemics despite a layered haze of smoke and steam that rose from the floor to the ceiling. Dr. ——— gave them away. He was naked and slouched over an enormous martini at a table on the far side of the saloon. He sipped the martini with a straw and stared at his lap. Achtung 66.799 fluttered his eyes until he had zoomed in to an extreme close-up on the plaquedemic's face→ → → →No expression save a subtle frown and a bead of liquid flowing down his chin. He snapped a photo, zoomed back out. And closed in...

Voss Winkenweirder sat across from Dr. ———. Had to be Dr. Identity. It dressed in a zoot suit whose fabric was a patchwork of handheld and compact mirrors. Penny-sized mirrorshades covered its eyes. Its neoElvis hairdo was a lard-laden wall that rose out of its forehead and seemed to dare people to try and knock it over. Its facemask contained the trademark Winkenweirder chin, distinguished by a trilogy of bullethole dimples, as well as the movie star's celebrated wingtip cheekbones, which had won four Hackademy Awards for Best Facial Feature. Unlike its companion, the android sat erect, smoking a long, sentient cigar. The cigar squeaked and squirmed in agony upon each inhalation. Achtung 66.799 zoomed, snapped...Now if he could get Dr. Identity to take off its mask...

He bypassed lion tamers and disco dancers. He ducked flying shuriken and shrunken heads. He stepped over the thrashing limbs of orgiastics. Stench of raw sex. Taste of dry ice...

Achtung 66.799 wondered why the plaquedemics retreated into the Schizoverse. To conceal themselves? If so, why wasn't Dr. ——— incognito? It didn't make sense.

He stopped in his tracks. What if the Ids didn't belong to the plaquedemics at all? Maybe the Id that resembled Dr. ——— was just another Id dressed up as Dr. ———'s Id. It was possible. The massacre at Corndog University had only occurred that morning. But incalculable paraphernalia created in both plaquedemics' images were already for sale. T-shirts, action figures, cereals, jetpacks, keychains, cigarettes, cologne, hairdos, jewelry, paper goods, weapons, press-on eyelashes and fingernails, household cleaners and appliances—all products carried the plaquedemics' brand name. No reason why the plaquedemics' Ids wouldn't be for sale, too. At the same time, Achtung 66.799 didn't see any other Dr. ———s. Nor did he see any Dr. Identities. The absence worried him. But it probably meant that the doctors were authentic.

He moved forward again, sidestepping an angry, musclebound feminId that tried to karate chop him. She muttered something in Schizospeak. Her dialect was a polylinguistic stream of technojargon and rhizomatics. Achtung 66.799 only understood bits and pieces of it.

He smiled innocently at her.

The feminId flexed her pectoral muscles and growled a metallic growl. Her nippleless fake breasts leapt to stony attention. Throbbing black veins consumed the surface of her ashen skin. A few of the veins burst. Spurting, gushing cords thrashed in the wounds. She got even madder.

He squeaked at her.

She said something else in Schizospeak, this time totally unintelligible.

Somebody elbowed Achtung 66.799 in the back. He looked behind him.

The Id was a replica of President-thing Grimley Bogue and stared at him as if in a trance.

"Yes?"

The Id broke out of his trance, frowned as if insulted, and disappeared into a large cluster of Fruit-of-the-Loom characters and feminIds in flapperwear.

Flustered, Achtung 66.799 looked at his antagonist.

She had nabbed another passerby and put him in a headlock. The Id's face was purple, almost black from suffocation. When the head snapped off, it burst into confetti and his body melted and frothed away.

The feminId emitted a Tarzan hogcall.

For a moment Achtung 66.799 thought about pretending she wasn't there. Maybe she wasn't there in the first place. Maybe she was a hallucination. Hallucinations were common phenomena in the Schizoverse experienced regularly by nearly forty percent of users. This further problematized the Papanazi's ultimate objective: the plaquedemics might not be there either. But if he started questioning the metaphysical validity of everything, how could he function? He had to assume the worst, which is to say, he had to assume that even potential fictions were real.

He said, "Pardon me, ma'am. I'm sorry if I offended you. I have to use the toilet. Excuse me." He took off like a road runner...

...and went down like Wile E. Coyote.

14

excerpt from "the post(post)/post-post+postmodern icklyophobe: ultra/counter\hyper-nihilism in fiona birdwater's megaanti-micronovel, *the ypsilanti factor*" – 1st person ('blah)

...elided a dialogically problematized ludic that Gretle and her entourage of xenophobes entirely lacked the psychocratic ability to cognize. This figuration of conjugated subjectivity not only produces a detached awareness of molecularized perception in the fictional characters of the novel's post(post)/ post-post+postmodern diegetic megahyperreality, it produces a detached awareness of molarized perception in the creative nonfictional characters of the novel's (post)/post-post+postmodern readers, whose actually acute megahyperreality is thus retroactively transfigured into a figurative scarecrow whose "spitshined phalanges gleam in the light of the winking, winedark moon" (Cantaloupe 294).

[9,341] This dynamic references a point I made earlier in regard to the function of Xanadu Booberry and her interpellation into the icklyophobic system of ethics to which I have subjected my decidedly polygonal hermeneutic of suspicion. *The Ypsilanti Factor* underscores a much deeper mediumessage than that which is suggested by the former reinscription of Big Bad White (She)Male syndrome. Booberry's "desire to reclaim a sense of multiperspectival selfhood" is a mere simulated emotive mechanism whereby protagonist #16 conveys a particular mechanized image of its beep-beep subjectivity in the eyes of the Department of Infocojack as much as its own dereconstructed self (Legume 35). Hence the appearance of the kitschy Julio Iglesias simulacrum in

the 403rd chapter. Recall the simulacrum's physiognomy, namely its indexical jawline, joint-action nose and monological eyeballs, all of which reflect the very logocentric fertilizer that Booberry discharges from virtually every orifice. The metaphysics of presence effectuated by this instance of "renegade, mitochondriacal behavior" elicits a more perfunctory (albeit performative) rule of "Tommygun" thumb at work in the novel, that is, the *lebenswelt* of protagonist #8 and #29 that I discussed in paragraph 220 is likewise inscribed upon the social and ideological body of the "doppelgängster" in question (Artichoke 67, 101). I will return to this digression in paragraph 10,035. For now, let us focus on the character of Birdwater herself as she manifests in the form of a sentient tomato who Booberry must slice, salt and consume.

[9,342] Birdwater as tomato is a flaming law of contradiction in which an analog communication erupts like a fistful of aporia. The general hermeneutics of this embodiment are as palpable as a slap in the face on a cold, wet morning. Doubtless Birdwater is revising the curious nature of tomatohood by reconfiguring its global misperception. The characters that populate the matrix of *The Ypsilanti Factor* mistakenly regard the fictional Birdwater, a tomato, to be a fruit when in fact she is a vegetable, unlike the characters that populate our own diegetic reality—that is, unlike me and you—who, broadly speaking, categorize the tomato as a vegetable when it is in fact a fruit. All this is unbalanced by the personification of the tomato in the novel—especially when we consider this act of personification as an act of persecution. The matter is further problematized in that the personified/ persecuted tomato does not move, talk, sing, or indicate in any way that it is an organism possessing intellect, emotion, and other so-called humanlike qualities. Indeed there is a terribly real chance the tomato that is a fictional representation of Fiona Birdwater is not sentient at all but rather a "vegetable" the likes of which one might find in the grocery store socializing with other dirt-born provisions. Thus any ethnomethodology of the "vegetable" in question invokes a logical paradox and, interpreted from a schizopatriarchal gaze, has the capacity to wield a revolutionary ideoverse by dint of the nature of such an

apodictic truth. Whatever the genuine pseudonature of the tomato (or tomatoes in general), however, Booberry must confront the "veritable Martian," as it were, and subject it to a partial ontological erasure (Birdwater 889). It is only when Booberry accomplishes this erasure that an operable borderzone (albeit not in a Lyotardian sense) is partially armageddoned. Consider the following passage:

> He walks into the kitchen and turns on the lights. He yawns. There is a tomato sitting on the edge of the counter. He shuffles across the floor and picks up the tomato. He looks at it. He places it on a cutting board.
>
> "Xanadu?" says a voice from another room. "Tomorrow is Wednesday."
>
> He nods in dark understanding. He removes a knife from a drawer. He slices the tomato in half. It bleeds Spaghetti sauce. Pressing together his lips, he reaches for the salt. (59)

The autopoetic unity visible in this sequence is the pathological product of its structural coupling. One gleans a sense of patterned jello here that hints at a mere post+postmodern aesthetic. This is canny subterfuge on Birdwater's part, particularly in light of the koinonia that exists between Booberry, the tomato and the voice. Note how the voice lacks a body. The voice is furthermore discharged "from another room." Such a disjunction is both intended to derange readers[118,021] while figuratively reifying the triangulation that classifies this work not as a post+postmodern phenomenon, but as a post-post+postmodern and post(post)/post-post+postmodern phenomenon at one and the same time.

[9,343] Thus far my theoretical blitzkrieg has focused mainly on establishing an operational definition of the paramodal narrative technique that distinguishes *The Ypsilanti Factor*. I have also attempted to demarcate the coordinates of this novel within the *commedia del foul* genre considering

---

118,021 In a recent interview on channel 44,506's *The Red Sky at Morning Show*, Birdwater explained how her intention in writing this sequence was literally to "induce a state of apelike psychosis in readers, if only on a marginal level."

the frequency with which its protagonists endeavor to woo and marry chickens. However, I have yet to broach the ultra/counter\nihilistic vibrations that distinguish the novel as a postpositivist, unilateral instance of catachresis that challenges the acausal principles of the inscribing socius and calls for the death of language in general. I hope to accomplish this feat by the end of this essay. If the feat is not accomplished, I officially reserve the right to do so in another essay that I shall tentatively entitle "The Post(post)/post-post+postmodern Icklyophobe: Ultra/counter\hyper-nihilism in Fiona Birdwater's Megaanti-micronovel, *The Ypsilanti Factor*—The Sequel." In the meantime, I want to revert to the critically acclaimed Hillbilly Scatman Goes To Lunch scene in which there is a "periodizing (mis)disaf(in)fect(a)tion" of "immanent, hamburgler temporality" on the "specters of the (megahyper)diaperreal" and their impact on the "historiographic sublimation of the abyss of reversal's informatic penchant for apocalypticism and ethical cybernetymology."[118,022] Prior to the injection of this scene into Birdwater's textual flesh, said flesh is a mere tapestry of whale blubber onto which has been imprinted only the vague likeness of some form of semantic use-value. In other words, the novel fails to transcend its jejune *Dasein*, relegating itself to an oligophrenic, isomorphic, rasorial and above all limaceous vapulation with a bad case of cardialgia that promulgates a gongoozling, idiotropic battology at best.[118,023]

[9,344] Patrique O'Darkness has argued that the general character and social performativation of Hillbilly Scatman is "a retroFreudian symptom of a sociosymboeconomic homosexual desire for the Names-of-the-Father in a

---

118,022 Save the first citation, which I appropriated from Kingsley E. Fella's *Cannibals, Tonka Trucks, and the Death of Abjection: A Study of Dialectic Indiscretions in East African Pigmy Haiku*, all citations in this sentence have their origins in scholarly articles on Birdwater's fiction. These articles are, respectively, "Transcoded Meliorisms, The Ghost of Ike Turner and Fiona Birdwater's *The Beaker Factor*" (3,004), "Schiz-Freuds of *The Gooseflesh Factor*" (2), and "'My Name Is Birdwater': Solipsism and Assholery in Mz. Birdwater's *The Birdwater Factor*" (346).

118,023 Many of the terms employed in this sentence were abstracted from Peter Bowler's *The Superior Person's Book of Words* (1979). See Bowler's seminal text for extended definitions and illustrations.

literal sense. This would explain why the Hillbilly consistently scribbles his step-father's real name and aliases on pieces of scrap paper and ejaculates on them. These closet spectacles of would-be *jouissance* are often followed by moments of extreme public defecation that are particularly curious and revealing" (67). Jean-Claude Biff and Antoine Formaldehyde take a less direct approach, claiming Scatman is a product of "the stalwart functionalism that typifies his daily life. He produces semen because he is a producing-machine. He produces excrement for the same reason. It's not complicated, folks" (*Fungulations* 444n). Others attribute this behavior to the fact that he was not spanked as a child but rather forced to endure a surplus of time-outs. The latter is the most popular view. My view is an altogether divergent animal. What critics have failed to recognize is that Hillbilly Scatman is a bivalent mechanical alien created and inserted into the social matrix by actual aliens from the planet Mowgli. If one were to peel him like a grapefruit, one would not encounter something juicy and pink beneath the surface but rather something more like the guts of a flybike. Put differently, he is not a man. Or, if he is a man, indeed, it is only insofar as his ideology operates under the aegis of a Nietzschean *joie de vivre* and *fin de siècle* technosocioeconomic attitude. Some might argue that this *de rigueur* claim is a natural, potentially ecological corollary to my staunch *bête noire façon de vivre*. They might say it is a *dernier cri* on my part to salvage an *à la carte* argument that relies solely on *trompe l'oeil* and that may or may not be *entrée dans le shitter*, if you will. After all, Nietzsche did explain early in *Ecce Homo*, his penultimate work, that he was, while anthropomorphous, "more akin to a stick of dynamite than a human being."[118,024] In any event, Scatman is a heterotopic freak of (in)human anti-nature that imbricates the laws of rationality and coerces readers to rethink the anti-nature of (in)human paralogical utterances.

[9,345] Hillbilly Scatman is an invasive presence in *The Ypsilanti Factor* whose slippery-when-wet *raison d'être* and unreasonable troublemaking

---

118,024   From the "Boomstick Translation" of *Ecce Homo*, pg. 4.

inform the modus operandi of numerous protagonists (e.g. #4, #8, #17, #23 and #24). I would not go so far as to call him a protagonist himself as the spirit of protagonism requires a certain "pancreatic symbology" that he altogether lacks.[118,025] Additionally, he suffers from gymnophobia and usually hides behind large objects in fear of the notion that his clothes might suddenly fall off and expose the world to his nakedness, the sight of which, he suspects, would turn onlookers into brain-eating zombies. This affliction is significant in terms of the aforementioned Goes To Lunch scene as it is the only point in the story where Scatman does not conceal his body in some quixotic fashion, albeit he considers the prospect on occasion. The scene reads:

A cat crossed the Hillbilly's path as he adjusted the suspenders of his overalls and clamored towards the front door of the bistro. The cat had dark purple fur and went "Meow!" four times. Taken aback, the Hillbilly clutched his chest. He became lightheaded and, thinking he might pass out, carefully lay down on the ground so that, if he did pass out, he wouldn't hit his head. A mechanical Chinaman with overexaggerated facial features pulling a politician wearing a top hat and monocle in a rickshaw ran him over. So did a number of pedestrians. Realizing he wasn't going to lose consciousness, the Hillbilly stood up, brushed the tire marks and footprints off of his overalls, and entered the bistro.

"Ahhhhhh!" exclaimed a maître d' from behind a tall podium. The Hillbilly glanced suspiciously over his shoulders. Was the exclamation a reaction to his unannounced presence? He apologized despite himself, eyeballing a nearby statue that seemed just large enough to hide his body from view.

The maître d' smiled, then used what looked like a mascara brush to pencil a thin mustache onto his towering overlip. The Hillbilly waited for him patiently. In the background, waiters and busboys ran

118,025   For more on what constitutes protagonism, see Poindexter Rearguard's *Protagonism, Constipation and Civilization: A Guide to Sentient Literature.*

at top speed from table to table, taking orders and serving food. Now and then a busboy paused, dumped a bucket of dirty plates and glasses onto the floor, tapdanced on the mess, and shot himself in the head with a pistol. Another busboy promptly descended from the rafters on puppet strings to take the dead one's place, making sure to clean the carcass up with the broken dinnerware that had been forsaken.

Inspecting the mustache with a hand mirror, the maître d' wiped it off of his face five times, unhappy with its appearance. Finally he settled on one. "Name please?"

The Hillbilly began to sweat. "I don't think I remember," he said.

The maître d' huffed. "I'm terribly sorry, sir, but we don't seat diners who either lack or fail to articulate their names. Is this a hardship with which you are familiar?"

Panicked, the Hillbilly took a step towards the statue. He stopped himself before he could take a second step.

"Scatman?" he said. "My name is Mr. Scatman." A dove flew out of his beard.

The maître d' looked at the dove disapprovingly. "Fine, Mr. Scatman. I might add that the bistro upholds a No Pets Allowed policy. Failure to comply must inevitably result in the death of the errant pet that is brought onto these grounds by the felonious party. Do you understand?"

"No," said the Hillbilly, frowning.

Unwilling to pursue the matter further, the maître d' pushed a button on the podium. A faceless robot wearing a tall, neon orange hunter's cap emerged from a secret door in the wall and riddled the sky of the bistro full of holes with a machine gun. After a short pause, the dove fell to the floor along with a few busboys. The robot saluted the maître d' and disappeared back into the wall.

"We apologize for the inconvenience, good sir," remarked the maître d', "but you must understand that a policy is not something one can easily skirt, ignore or disgrace. Table for one?"

Still not understanding, the Hillbilly shook his head compliantly and allowed the maître d' to escort him to a table. For a moment he considered crawling under the table—maybe a waiter would serve him down there?—but he resolved to take the opposite route and sat on top of it, his legs hanging over the edge, the tips of his boots scraping against the floor. He lunched on a salad of sauerkraut and caramel-coated lima beans that he ate out of his lap, then snuck out of the bistro without paying the bill.

The police apprehended him.

They stripped his cloths off in the interrogation room. It was at this point, for the first time, that the Hillbilly's purpose in life struck him between the eyes like a crucifixion nail. (Birdwater 126-127)

The allopathic, psychogeographic, dromological implications of this scene are obvious enough, and the messianic legitimation of Hillbilly Scatman as allegorical martyr is egregious to a disaffectingly relativistic degree. The scene, in other words, speaks for itself in terms of its situational catachresis, not to mention the highly overspecialized way in which Birdwater partakes in a correspondence theory of truth here. I am admittedly hesitant to pursue a discussion of Scatman in the above context, partly because of the immediately aforementioned point(s), partly because of the point(s) I made earlier in this essay (which, to reiterate, I will return to in due course). This elicits the question of why I cited or even mentioned the Goes To Lunch scene, which has little or nothing to do with any of my originary theses. The answer is...

15
the briefcase – 3rd person

A man opened a pink Big Chill Retro vintage refrigerator and removed a carton of plain yogurt. He opened the carton. He sniffed the yogurt. He sniffed it again.

He vomited in the kitchen trough.

Inside of a pyroelectric wine glass sitting on the counter stood the miniaturized holographic image of a telecaster reciting the morning news in a high-pitched squeak. The telecaster's hairdo was a burning orange bush. The flames blackened and his voice slipped into a baritone as a newsflash threaded into his monologue. "This just in. Holocaust at Corndog University. Plaquedemics dead. Student-things dead. Madcap behavior. Perpetrators suspected to be plaquedemics. One human, one 'gänger. Good-looking. Fair sense of style. At large. Pigs on the scene. Papanazi on alert. Ultraviolence, gore. Stay tuned."

The man cleaned his mouth with a damp washcloth.

He opened a closet and turned on his 'gänger. "Zippity do da," it said.

"Mr. Bogarty 2," said the man, and retired to the bathroom to masturbate.

Mr. Bogarty 2 adjusted and dusted off its suit, made a cup of coffee, took a sip, gargled, spit it out, picked up a briefcase, made sure the briefcase was locked, and left.

The 2,450 story elevator ride to the ground floor of the spacescraper took fifteen minutes. The elevator only stopped once. A half-naked oldster got on. Slung over his shoulder was a knapsack of Legos. He emptied them onto the floor, kneeled, and hurriedly built a small castle. He didn't exit the elevator

143

when they touched down.

Mr. Bogarty 2 worried about its tie as it hopped onto a slideway. Next to it was a 'gänger who had on a superior tie in its opinion. Its fingers tightened around the handle of the briefcase.

The slideway curled into a funhouse tunnel. Clowns, demons, smurfs, pornstars, Babars, homunculi, Pee-Wee Hermans danced and battled on the ceiling screens. The slideway sped up, jerked left, skated right, spiraled upwards...Momentum and magnetism kept most of the riders in place. A few flew off into the Void.

The slideway slowed down, smoothed out and emerged back into the open. It was high above ground level now, suspended in the air by interminable, pencil-thin copper wires that stretched into the sky.

A vidship passed overhead. The megascreen on its underside ran footage of an ultraviolent scikungfi fight. The camera moved in on a bloody, twitching victim. A clawlike appendage removed the victim's mask...exposing the face of Voss Winkenweirder. The camera zoomed in to a close-up→→→→His face was bruised, dripping. A gray tongue hung out of his mouth. For streetgoers with 3D glasses or vision, a holographic image of the tongue drooped out of the vidship's bottom and swung across the slideways. "Movie star killed by plaquedemic menace," whirred the vidship. It repeated the announcement and urged people to beware of university educators of any kind until further notice.

Mr. Bogarty 2 momentarily forgot about ties. Its eyes functioned in realspace and 3D at the same time and the swinging tongue disoriented it. Then the android's focus returned to its tie and the tie's lack of stylistic gumption, at least in comparison with the tie wrapped around the neck of the android at its side. It bit its lip, staring at the rival fashion statement out of the corners of two white, bulbous eyes.

"It's a fine unit," declared Mr. Bogarty 2 in a defeated tone.

The 'gänger didn't hear it.

"I say. It's a fine unit."

The 'gänger turned and regarded Mr. Bogarty 2. "Sexuality is not part of my program. I'm sorry."

Something snapped in Mr. Bogarty 2. It started talking in Voodoospeak as if possessed. It uttered a mélange of deep, robotic sounds. Then it toppled backwards. Its eyes popped out of its head on springs and all of its limbs broke into furious convulsions.

Ignoring the death throes, the 'gänger picked up Mr. Bogarty 2's briefcase and coolly exited the slideway...

"Good morning, Herr Kincain," said a receptionist to the 'gänger on its approach to the front desk. A giant cockroach, the receptionist had a Betty Davis head sticking out of its midsection. The head was black-and-white except for the bright red lipstick smeared over its lips. An old-fashioned switchboard hung on the wall—a tangle of wires, buttons and levers. The receptionist used her legs to fiddle with the contraption as she played greeter and answered phone calls.

Herr Kincain smiled at the receptionist without saying anything. On the radio the voice of an irate newscaster was in the middle of a diatribe: "They have no use-value! They're not scientists. They're not lawyers. They're not fucking psychologists. They're not even anthropologists. They're goddamned English professors! *Philologists.* The lowest form of plaquedemic, in this pundit's opinion, next to the philosopher and the historian. It's no wonder they're committing holocausts everywhere they go. They serve no postcapitalist purpose. They believe in nothing but their novels and their punctuation marks..."

"That's a lovely tie, Herr Kincain," the receptionist noted as the android waited for an elevator.

Herr Kincain glanced down at the tie. "A lovely tie," it echoed.

Twenty minutes later a bell chimed and the elevator doors creaked open.

A wave of bodies spilled out of the cabin and washed over Herr Kincain. Holding the briefcase tightly, it struggled to maintain balance and stay on its feet. But the wave was too powerful. It lost its footing, tumbled over, and got trampled.

The last thing it saw before passing out: the elevator conductor's smiling pinhead, which loomed over him and began to inflate like a balloon...

Shrieking, the receptionist leapt over the front desk and scuttled towards the body of Herr Kincain.

The elevator conductor snatched the briefcase and ducked back into the cabin. He pressed the button for the 3,002nd floor, massaging the skin of the briefcase like the thighs of an expensive hooker...

The elevator stopped at the 3rd floor. Two neozooters stepped on. They were having a conversation in Donaldduckspeak.

As the doors closed, a bandit wearing a Zorro mask and cape leapt onto the elevator and punched out all three occupants. He pushed the emergency button and robbed them of their wallets, jewelry and eyeballs...

A special report cut off the elevator Muzak. "Pardon the interruption, citizens of Bliptown. The Bullsheet News Institute offers the following update on recent holocausts committed by the now infamous Corndog plaquedemics: they are still on the loose and acting like sons of bitches. The Winkenweirder camp has increased the bounty on their heads from one to *three* lifetime memberships at Littleoldladyville on the condition that these additional memberships are assigned to alternate personalities only. Bring the doctors in dead or alive and you, too, can be a psychotically satisfied shopper."

The bandit tore out the last pair of eyeballs and stuffed them in his satchel. He stood up, threw the satchel over his shoulder, turned to leave... and saw the briefcase. Giggling, he grabbed it, exited the elevator, and ran at top speed down a long hallway. At the end was a tall window. He wore hightop jetshoes and the resonance of his giggling increased with his speed as he bowled over the businesspeople that fastwalked across the hallway from one office to another.

He accelerated to 60 mph by the time he exploded through the window.

Every hour was rush hour in Bliptown and the flyways were a deafening maze of propulsion. The bandit sailor-dived a mile down, playfully dodging traffic, then clicked together the heels of his jetshoes. They morphed into manta rays. The rays' wings parachuted open, broke his fall, flipped him upright and held him steady. The bandit's Zorro cape split up the back, unleashing a set of tremendous, fake-looking Condor wings. He had recently stolen the wings from the set of the film *Condorman VII: Condorman vs. The Greatest American Hero*, which was being shot near his luxury conapt in Bliptown's Vagina Light district. Tucking the briefcase into his armpit, he flapped the wings at a hummingbird's speed and zipped away...

He landed on a rooftop featuring a cheap, outdoor massage parlor. There was also a golfing range, a small square of Astroturf on which arcane men and 'gängers wearing Hawaiian shirts and white pants stood shoulder-to-shoulder trying to hit balls as hard as they could. For the most part, they whiffed and hit each other: half of them clutched their bodies and moaned in pain. Every now and then, though, a golfer made contact and sent a ball sailing into the depths of Bliptown's mechanical dystopiascape...

The bandit descended onto a small landing strip. His jetshoes morphed back into hightops and his wings caved into his cape. He let the briefcase fall out of his armpit and caught it by the handle. Cracking his neck, he strode towards the massage parlor. It was busy but there were two open massage tables. Behind them two naked, airbrushed female 'gängers waited patiently to rub him down and jerk him off.

A tabloid bug landed on his shoulder. "Heard the latest news? Dr. Identity is actually a highly intelligent ostrich in disguise. And the bird has fleas!"

The bandit glared at the bug, a common housefly except for a set of thick, chapped human lips that lay in front of it like two pink slugs sleeping one atop the other. The lips frothed with mucous. What appeared to be a salamander leg stuck out of their jagged crease. The fly's speaking voice belonged to a veteran stage actor. "There's more," it continued. "Dr. ——— teaches his student-things that a split infinitive is a verb afflicted with schizophrenia. He also believes verbs have feelings and should be nurtured accordingly. Nouns, on the other hand, are lifeless, unempathetic organisms, he says."

Frowning, the bandit flicked the bug in the lips. The bug cried out as it tumbled away and tried to steady itself with long, oily wings. It landed on its back, legs flailing.

The bandit stomped on it.

His muscles tensed and he dropped the briefcase. The bug's stinger had slid through the sole of his jetshoe, piercing his foot and injecting him with a microtoxin that produced a mortal desire to buy a copy of *The Daily Assfuck*. The microtoxin didn't agree with his genetic makeup and also produced an unfortunate side effect: nipples sprouted all over his body. A few of the nipples were accompanied by breasts, one of which formed on his cheek and began to lactate.

The bandit had been a sociopath. The nipples rendered him a psychotic. He shed his clothes and wings and began to tear the nipples from his body, scratching and ripping them off with his nails. His body became a sprinkler of blood and milk. The golfers stopped swinging their clubs and stared quizzically at him. So did several masseuses and loitering cow-pigeons.

He staggered towards the edge of the roof, bounded along the rim, and toppled over...

The massage parlor and golfing range sat atop a vidbuilding. Currently one of its megascreens showed a reenactment of the holocaust in which Dr. Identity murdered Voss Winkenweirder. The bandit's silhouette was a black tear that streamed down the vast cheek of the megascreen...

The reenactment was a live performance. The director yelled cut and broke into view. The camera zoomed into his head→→→→which flaunted a Broom Hilda hairdo and scores of broken blood vessels. "Holocaust at Littleoldladyville! The plaquedemics are striking again, folks, at this very moment. This time they mean business!" The camera cut to a nosebleeder view of a gnat-sized Dr. Identity tearing apart various gnat-sized Babettas and BEMs. The scene dithered as the Papanazi filming it picked his nose.

The director's face reappeared. "We're prepared to bring this live holocaust to you right now, live squared, even as it unfolds," he boomed. "Places everybody! Places!" The camera zoomed out and the greenscreen on the set assumed the background of Littleoldladyville as the actors who had been reenacting the Winkenweirder-related holocaust changed costumes and darted back and forth in preparation for the new, realtime enactment. Ten seconds later the director's voice bellowed, "Hacktion!!!" Most of the actors were still squirming into BEM suits and screwing on Babetta heads. But the actor playing Dr. Identity attacked anyway, barraging them with rubber throwing stars and knives...

The briefcase lay on the rooftop for over an hour. Either nobody noticed it or nobody cared about it.

A cow-pigeon lurched over. Tentatively the bird stuck out its tongue and licked the skin of the briefcase. It tasted all right. The bird pecked at the briefcase, trying to bore a hole in it, but the skin was too thick, so it tried to pick the lock with its talons. When that failed it clamped the handle with its beak, emitted a muffled *Mooooooo!*, and clumsily fluttered into the sky.

While cumbersome and goofy-looking, cow-pigeons were fast, given enough space to accelerate. Some ornithologists and amateur birdwatchers referred to them as the cheetahs of the sky, clocking them at over 70 mph on occasion. This particular cow-pigeon, however, was old and had a bum wing: its speed topped out at 7 mph. It seemed to be swimming underwater as it loped across the unfriendly skies of Bliptown, vehicles and alaristrians threatening its life at every turn.

A few balls of excrement escaped the cow-pigeon. Most of them smashed into windshields and caused gruesome accidents, but one managed to make the long journey to the street, landing on the head of a Kevin Bacon clone. It was a human—and a public anomaly. Shortly after the real movie star's death, a community of Hungarian scientists, who, in addition to teaching neurobiology at Johannes Yobbery University, had also presided over the European branch of the Kevin Bacon Fan Club, decided to clone the actor in an effort to keep the dream alive, as it were. Unable to stop at one, they cloned thousands. People started to worry. For a time there seemed to be more Kevin Bacons (and Kevin Bacon 'gängers) in the world than actual non-Kevin Bacon life forms. A holocaust ensued and the Bacons were almost entirely liquidated. Now a near extinct species, they were hardly ever seen in public, preferring to live amongst themselves in remote subterranean Batcaves.

Man or machine, the Kevin Bacons came in many guises and ages, depending upon the character in the film they were patterned after. This one was a *Footloose* Bacon, the most popular model: Staticelectric hairdo, wife-thing-beater T-shirt, skintight Wranglers and cowboy boots. He had been telling off a street performer. The street performer boasted a cheap Dr. Identity mask and may or may not have been an actual 'gänger. Using flashy, poorly executed Karate Kid moves, it pretended to kill strangers as they passed by. An out-of-control swan kick accidentally connected with Kevin Bacon's shoulder. Infuriated, the clone threatened to sue the street performer, shaking his fists, performing angry dance moves, and reciting lines from *Footloose* in his defense, his favorite line being, "The music is on my side."

Then the cow-pigeon's shit tagged him.

The force of the blow nailed the Bacon's body a few inches into the street. His neck broke on impact and he slumped over and died. The street performer poked at the corpse with his toes. Satisfied, he removed his mask and exposed a *Tremors* Bacon...

The cow-pigeon loped on...After a while it grew tired and landed on the upside of an airworm that was stopped at a traffic light. A Smaug Turbo GT tore across an overhead flyway. A throng of rampant Papanazi tailed it...

The cow-pigeon lay its head down on the briefcase. It fell asleep and dreamt that it was young again, with strong wings, a full mane of hair, lively udders and a bright white grin...

Taking a sharp turn, the airworm twisted onto its side. The bird and the briefcase slid off.

The bird never woke up.

The briefcase landed in the back seat of a convertible Beauford with streamers of crepe paper and strings of empty beer cans flowing in its train. A newly married husband and wife-thing sat in the front seat. The husband fumbled with the knobs of the car's vintage Blaupunkt radio, trying to find a station that played Hee-Haw. But the same thing was on every channel: "Holocausts are sparking up in multiple...sectors at the same time...Either the plaquedemics are cytokinetic organisms...who are splitting apart like... mitotic cells or...they have developed the capacity to move from place to place...at the speed of light, unleashing their queer brand of Terror...Half the population of Bliptown...is dead...clinically insane...or seriously concerned about their psychosomatic welfare. Local...military...forces...are...in the process...of smashing down the city walls...and allowing...the fictional monsters...who inhabit the surrounding...rainforests to...invade our...great metropolis...It may be Bliptown's only chance..."

"Goddamn this thing!" The husband punched the radio, breaking off one of its knobs.

"That's mature," said the wife-thing.

"Mind your hole!"

Casting her hair over her shoulder, the wife-thing noticed the briefcase. She unfastened her belt, climbed halfway over the seat and fumbled for it. It was almost out of reach. Her backside nudged the husband.

"Move your fat ass!"

Finally she got hold of the briefcase, sat back down and put it in her lap. She eyed the husband. "What's this?"

The husband eyed her back. "That's my briefcase, bitch!" he shouted. Keeping one hand on the wheel, he tried to confiscate it.

The wife-thing held on tight. "What's this? What's this? What's this?" she kept saying. The Beauford bounced and shook as the couple struggled.

The husband slammed on the brakes. The wife-thing's head smacked into the glove compartment, crushing her veil and breaking her nose. Blood poured from her nostrils. She bawled and gurgled. The husband yanked the briefcase out of her grasp and lifted it over his head, victorious...

A carpmobile rear-ended the Beauford. Both vehicles exploded. The briefcase was projected six blocks away on a spout of fire.

151

Dr. Identity

The fire died out. The briefcase lost altitude and plummeted, plummeted, plummeted...Three minutes later it receded into a deep, abandoned alleyway that functioned both as a landfill and a graveyard for citizens who couldn't afford to incinerate, cryogenize or reincarnate their loved ones. Piles of rotten, steaming humans and 'gängers and garbage stretched as far as the eye could see...

The briefcase landed on a scavenging armadillo, crushing it. The skin of the briefcase was burnt and damaged. But its lock remained tightly fastened.

Nearby an old Truetone television set came to life. Behind the lines of static that played jazz on its screen was a clip of Dr. Identity using a samurai sword to cut the heads off of a gang of Dr. Identity lookalikes. The clip moved in slowtime and played over and over and over...

An hour later, talk show host Fibb Defibrillator pushed his fingers into the static and opened it like a curtain. A blinding grin leapt out of his golden bust. "Good afternoon. I'm Fibb Defibrillator. It doesn't get much worse than this, folks. Dr. Identity and his cowardly plaquedemic Real McCoy continue to take advantage of the good people of Bliptown with unabashed determination. I'm here to tell you that something must be done soon. If they remain on the lam, no doubt the Media, the Law, and ultimately the General Public will tire of them. Their dirty deeds will go unchecked, and no matter what they do, they will exist as invisible ghosts on the megascreen of history..."

16
schizoverse, part 2 – 1st person (identity)

"Dr. Identity. I'm talking to you."

I prodded the stripper's breasts with my index finger. She stood there patiently as I studied the protrusions. The absence of nipples perplexed me. Even I had nipples.

"The narrative of my life is out of my hands, I said."

I nodded gravely at the stripper. Smoke leaked out of my nostrils. "I heard you."

"Did you? I'm curious."

"Drink your drink." Emotion flooded into the stripper's face. Her brow wrinkled as a surreptitious Id took her from behind.

I looked at Dr. 'Blah. "Your lack of nipples concerns me as well. Why do you insist on walking around with that lack? Why can't you put on a costume like real people?"

He lapped at his martini. "Costumes are for the birds. Real people are for the birds. Birds are for the birds."

I puffed on my cigar. The cigar yelped. I told it to pipe down. "Very funny," the cigar replied. I dropped it on the floor and stomped on it. Liquid ash sprayed out of either side of my boot sole.

The head of an Id standing behind Dr. 'Blah exploded. I couldn't determine if the head had been weaponized or went off of its own volition. Body shrapnel peppered Dr. 'Blah's scalp and shoulders. The shrapnel slid down his neck and then went up in smoke. He didn't seem to notice.

"I miss my student-things. Why did I forsake plaquedemia? Why? Why?"

"One why will suffice." I removed another cigar from my mirrorblazer. I strangled it to death before putting it in my mouth. "How long is this pity party going to last? Will it ever end? What can I do to make it end?"

"For starters, you can turn yourself in and tell the Pigs I had nothing to do with anything. I know I'll still be held responsible. But maybe then the Law won't torture me to death. A clean death is all I ask for. A soldier's death."

"Soldier? Are you serious?" A Bug-Eyed Monster cartwheeled by our table.

"Yes, actually."

I double-taked him. "That's not bad. At least you've retained a sense of humor." Another BEM cartwheeled by. This one struck me in the leg with a tendril.

"No I haven't. I'm on automatic pilot. I don't know what I'm saying. And I don't care."

"Horseshit. You care. You don't want to die. You don't want me to turn myself in. You certainly don't want to return to plaquedemia. Why can't you admit to yourself that what you want is precisely what's happened to you?" I spotted the third BEM on its approach. I grabbed it by an eye and lobbed it into the air and dropkicked it. The thing sailed across the saloon and struck a faceless Id wearing a ten foot trenchcoat in the chest. The Id fell backwards and a pair of stilts javelined into the ceiling. Cheers ensued.

Dr. 'Blah shook his head. "I didn't want this. I didn't want this."

"Yes you did. Yes you did."

An upside-down Id in a Land Shark suit swung overhead on a trapeze. Dr. 'Blah glanced absently at him. "I'm hungry."

"Eat something. Problem solved."

He hung his head. He fingered his martini. "I'm hungry."

A billow of orgiastics spilled into the saloon. They flowed onto the dance floor and began to assimilate ready-and-willing Ids and feminIds.

I looked Dr. 'Blah up and down. I pressed my lips together. "How dare you say you miss your student-things. But you'll see them again soon. Soon their 'gängers will be running the world."

Nearby a musclebound feminId picked up an endomorph in a *Wizard of Oz* flying monkey suit and tried to play it like a musical instrument. The monkey's tail stiffened as the feminId blew into the mouthpiece of its nose and pretended its vertebrae were the pistons of a trumpet.

"I don't understand some people," I said. "What drives some people to do the things they do?"

Dr. 'Blah gave me a dirty look. "I know what you're trying to do."

"I'm not trying to do anything."

"I don't agree."

"You have that right."

"I know I do."

I filled my cheeks with air. "Look. We're in the Schizoverse. In a saloon. There's pussy everywhere. You have a monstercock between your legs. Unstrap that monstercock and put it to use. If nothing else admire the freakery. Can't you at least try to have a little fun?"

"I don't care about pussy or monstercocks or freakery. I'm married. I have a wife-thing."

Consoling him was useless. "Fine. Be that way. I'm going to get a drink. Do you want anything?"

He glanced helplessly at me. His face was pale and waxen. "Don't leave me. I wouldn't know what to do with myself if I was by myself. I might get lonely." He reached over the table and gripped the handle of a mirror on my coat sleeve.

"Jesus." I took an angry puff of my cigar. Half its length seared to ash. I spit the smoke out of my ear holes. "Fine. I'll just stand here like an asshole and stare at things."

Another Id's head exploded.

Dr. 'Blah said, "Please, sit down." He politely gestured at the empty chair across from him. The tone in his voice had altered. It was more self-assured. It was downright friendly.

Dr. Identity

I said, "I don't want to sit down. Mind your own business and hope that a waitress comes by soon. Otherwise I'm spreading myself around this place. I'm not wearing this outfit for nothing."

Dr. 'Blah's head hung so low his chin dipped into his martini.

"Take your chin out of your drink."

A strange out-of-vogue brand of Beegee Muzak flared up. I couldn't place it. I peered over the heads of the disco dancers at the DJ. He was togged up in a John Travolta skinsuit and inflatable head. The gold chains and medallions hanging over the hairy V of his chest were so heavy that his body seemed like it might collapse from the weight. Yet his hands attacked the turntable with finesse. I mulled over killing him. My musical ear was sharp and stylized. But I wasn't in the mood to cause a ruckus. I wanted to relax. I wanted Dr. 'Blah to relax. Why was it so difficult for him to take a time out? He had been this way since he first purchased me. He had probably been this way his entire life. Anxiety defined his identity. The luge seemed to be his only comfort. And yet whenever he left the luge he seemed more anxious than ever.

Human. All too human...

A body crashed into the wall above us. It fell onto the tabletop and smashed Dr. 'Blah's martini.

"It hurts me inside," squeaked the Id. His facemask was scratched and bruised and torn. Dr. 'Blah seemed to recognize him. He knit his brow. His face lit up.

"Humidor?"

The Id's legs and arms and head hung limply off of the sides of the table. He lifted his head up. "That's me. Well, kinda." He tried to say something else but couldn't get it out. His head flopped back.

A flock of trenchers blew up and a feminId emerged from their electric ashes. It was the same feminId who had tried to turn the flying monkey into a trumpet. She flexed her pecs. She screamed at us in Schizospeak. She gestured towards the Id.

Dr. 'Blah stroked the Id's tattered forehead. He glanced at the feminId. Then at me. "Dr. Identity," he said. "If you please."

It was a refreshing command. My original had never asked me to kill somebody before. Simulated or otherwise.

I gave the feminId a taunting nod. This offended her and she abducted a passerby. She broke his back on her knee and tossed the body aside. Her expression begged me for an act of oneupmanship.

I cracked my neck.

The feminId raised an eyebrow.

I reached into my coat.

The feminId snapped into a scikungfi fighting stance.

I pulled out a Medusa Mirror.

The feminId grimaced in defeat.

The weapon was an upgrade and didn't merely turn her to stone when she gazed into it. It turned her inside out and bathed us in the black rain of her entrails...

"You're welcome," I said to 'Dr. Blah. He gazed at the passed-out Id with motherly concern. He looked worse than before. At the same time he looked better. A mysterious aura of spirituality outlined his body.

"Do you know who this is?"

I blinked at the Id. "A guy in an outfit?"

"No. Well, yes. But that's beside the point."

"Point?"

"It's Humidor Tang! One of my favorite writers and plaquedemics. I almost recreated myself in his image when I joined the faculty at Corndog University, you know. He teaches White Male Metawriting at the University of Shitforbrains in Cog City. I've been preparing to write an essay on his novel *Wichita George & the Case of the Spitshined Wingtips* for over a year now. It's a splendid piece of postvintage technodetective fiction."

"Splendid? What kind of word is that?"

Dr. 'Blah looked fiercely at me. "It's a word. Anyway, I've done enough research on the novel to write an entire book of criticism on it. I might be able to write an entire series of critical works on it."

"Sounds like a plan."

"Fuck you Identity! If it wasn't for you I could be writing about Tang right now, right this second!"

An Id in a cumbersome praying mantis suit crawled across the wall. He pardoned himself as he squeezed passed me. "Nobody's stopping you," I said to Dr. 'Blah. "Who's stopping you? You say you've been researching for over a year. Have you written one goddamn word yet? It's not my fault. I spend most of my time hanging in a fucking closet. What do you do?"

That quieted him. But I immediately felt guilty. Dr. 'Blah was such an easy target.

The fire in his eyes died out and he returned his attention to the Humidor Tang impersonator. "Please get me something to eat, Dr. Identity. I would appreciate that." He began to poke and flick the Tang in the cheek. "Wake up, sir," he whispered. "Wake up. Wake up."

On my way to the bar a trencher asked for my autograph. Its obese fedora hung down over the top half of its face and I could only perceive a shiteating Cheshire grin. The Id claimed to be a Voss Winkenweirder impersonator autograph collector and asked if I would sign my real name. I obliged. When it saw the name it tilted back its hat and ogled me. Its eyes were florescent eggs. Its face was a replica of movie star Voltaire Swingtime. The original Swingtime had once been lovers with the original Voss Winkenweirder. Was the 'gänger's original the original Swingtime? Perhaps I should ask it for an autograph...

"Is that *your* real name or an impersonation of a real name?" the Swingtime asked.

I shrugged. "I don't know. Goodbye." I started to walk away.

It grabbed me by the elbow. "Are you sure you don't know? I'd like to know."

"I'm sorry to hear that." I grabbed the 'gänger's face. I dug my thumb and index finger into its eye sockets. One powerful yank and the front half of its skull tore free. The oily machinery of its brains spilled out of its head. Then its trenchcoat fell to the floor in a lonely pile. Its fedora ascended into the fiery neon rafters of the saloon on broad wings of fabric...

I returned to the table ten minutes later with a basket of deep fried orphan hearts. The Tang sat across from Dr. 'Blah. Their conversation was overenthusiastic.

I didn't like it.

"I'm back."

"Now we can start the party," Dr. 'Blah sniggered. The Tang mimicked him.

"Here." I tossed the basket on the table. "Eat your hearts out."

They snubbed my pun. And the food. "Did you know the real Humidor Tang is a graduate of Giddyap State University?" tweeted Dr. 'Blah. "That's my alma mater! Tom Foolery here was just bringing me up to speed. Despite all of my research, it seems there's a great deal I don't know about Dr. Tang."

"Tom Foolery?"

The Id nodded. "Yup. That's me. I want to take this opportunity to thank you for saving my pseudolife back there. That was a close one."

"That was a close one," I repeated.

"Yup. Anyway, thanks." He stuck out his hand. I observed the hand and cocked my head. He kept the hand out. I kept observing it. I wondered how long he would leave it there.

Dr. 'Blah said, "Tang once spent two days out-city in a rain forest. Two days! He wanted to see if he could do it. Granted, he was well-protected by a militia of graduate students and teaching assistants who he had hypnotized, armed and ordered to protect him, but still, he made it. Rumor is he killed a Big Foot by ridiculing it to death. He also taught a Frankenstein monster how to play golf and read metaphysical poetry. That's the kind of plaquedemic I want to be. You should know, Dr. Identity, I'm going back. Back to plaquedemia. No matter what it takes. Once I square things with the Law, I'm changing my name again. I'm even getting plastic surgery this time. Soon I'll be a real Humidor Tang. And a real plaquedemic."

"A fine idea," I said politely. "Don't you think that's a fine idea?" I fixated on the Tang. Finally he let his hand drop onto the table. Behind me a Wayne Newton impressionist hit a high note.

"Whatever makes one happy," he replied. The Tang beamed at me. There was a suspicious flicker in his eyes.

It didn't take long to process and identify the flicker.

"You're about to die," I told the Tang. "We're all about to die." The Newton hit another high note. I roundhoused him in fasttime.

Dr. 'Blah tried to stand up. I stabbed him in the head with the handle of a mirror. Blood burbled from his mouth as he cursed me. He bit his tongue off. The tongue landed on the table and bounced into the Tang's lap. Dr. 'Blah liquefied...

I leered at the Tang. "Your turn, Papanazi."

He sighed. "Que será. It doesn't matter anyway. I got what I wanted."

"Maybe. Maybe not."

The Papanazi pulled out a vintage ray gun. I slapped it out of his hand. "I don't like guns. But I can appreciate a plethora of antique styles. Did you know that gun of yours was a replica of one that belonged to Starbuck in the original *Battlestar Galactica* television series? That actor who played Starbuck, Dirk Benedict, also appeared in the TV show *The A-Team* as a character named Face. The show was a quixotic piece of surrealism. Not only was it set in a non-science fictional universe, gunfights broke out all the time and nobody ever got killed. Can you believe it?"

He shook his head.

I ripped his head off.

As the head disintegrated I quickly thrust my hand into the neck hole and shortfused the photoreceptors inside. The Papanazi would have no pictures of us to take home to Big Brother when he reemerged into the real world. We would be seeing him again.

Pandemonium had broken out in the saloon. I gazed into the Medusa Mirror...

Dr. 'Blah yelled at me as my body rebuilt itself around the airy scaffolding of my Ego.

I removed the dildo from my cortical shunt and whacked him with it.

I told him how the Tang was a Papanazi. I told him he was stupid for not realizing it. I told him he was stupid for several other reasons. At last I told him he ought to shape up. "No more joyrides in the Schizoverse, got it?"

"You're the one that wanted to go! You're the one that was bored!"

"Whatever the case, that's that. You better get it together. Otherwise I don't know if we can be friends anymore."

Dr. 'Blah slouched. His chin began to quiver.

"Plaquedemia," he whispered...

17
dream of the brown lady – 1st person ('blah)

I had difficulty waking up as a child. When I fell into a deep enough sleep, I could remain indefinitely unconscious. Every morning my mother-thing had to drag me out of bed by the heels, pick me up by the shoulders, shake me like a rag doll, and scream in my face in order for me to regain consciousness. Once she resolved not to wake me to see how long I would stay asleep. She told me she wasn't going to wake me before I went to bed. "I think you might be a superhero," she said, glancing hesitantly across the room at the 'gänger of the man she was dating at the time. The 'gänger looked at me and sucked in its cheeks.

One night I awakened at 3:14 a.m.—unprovoked. I was five years old.

I slept on the bottom of a bunk bed. On top was my collection of action figures, stuffed animals and malformed papier-mâché dinosaurs, the latter of which I made in art class. I didn't like sleeping with them, but their proximity made me feel safe.

The bunk bed lay in a nook that extended into one corner of my bedcube. I had to enter the bed from a drop-drawer in its rear. About a half foot of space separated its edges from the walls. It was a claustrophobic's nightmare, but I liked tight spots. My favorite pastime was to have my mother-thing lock me in her trombone case and carry me around the house, pretending to be on her way to a concert. Accordingly I pretended to be her trombone.

I blinked at the chainmail undercarriage of the top bunk, then turned on my side and blinked at the wall.

My mother-thing had digigraffitied the whole room. Digigraffiti was one of her many illicit hobbies. For a while she made a living doing it, defacing the exterior of Bliptown as a freelance advertiser and Littleoldladyville-sponsored *artiste*. After a few run-ins with the Law, however, she gave it up, restricting herself to the interior of our cubapt.

My bedcube was a panorama of ultraviolence, an animated gorescape that my mother-thing continually updated, adding new characters and methods of slaughter. Fairy tale beasts, witches, giants, elves, dragons, princesses, mermen and Rumplestiltskins attacked, maimed, dismembered and ate each other in an apocalypse of zombified wrath and ruin. My mother-thing believed she was carrying out three positive objectives by creating such a spectacle. In order of importance, these were: 1) satisfying her nagging, overdramatized *artiste*'s desire to express her identity through the production of art; 2) entertaining (and in so doing educating) me; 3) preparing me for the absurdist, ultraviolent way of life that lay in wait for me in the real world.

The digigraffiti didn't entertain or educate me. It didn't scare me either. All the screaming and bloodshed and hellfire just annoyed me. Good thing I slept like a corpse.

An old-fashioned duel between a centaur and a satyr unfolded in the section of wall before me. Vintage German warplanes flew across the orange sky in the background as the characters systematically paced away from each other, pivoted, and fired muskets. Both creatures missed their targets. But the centaur had heat vision: two flaming rivers of lava beamed out of its eyes and doused the satyr, who, as it caught fire and began to melt, stopped, dropped and rolled. The centaur put an end to this safety measure, though, galloping over and trampling its victim with gigantic granite hooves. As it was reduced to mulch, the satyr swore and complained that it hadn't had enough time to live and accomplish its goals.

The centaur unleashed a piercing victory cry.

The Red Baron swooped out of a cloud and machinegunned the centaur in the back.

The centaur danced the dance of an electrified puppet as bullets riddled it.

The Red Baron climbed back into the sky, came around and dropped a bomb on the cadaver. An excess of blood and body parts and internal organs blew apart. The Red Baron beeped its horn and headed for the horizon where a flaming green sun was setting. The sun turned out to be a colossal worm with dreadlocks and a beard that rose out of the horizon, opened its fanged mouth, and devoured the warplane. Storm clouds moved in. A burst of acid rain perforated and cooked the body of the worm, and when the rain passed, a tribe of vicious Amelia Bedelia androids emerged from a cave and fell on the worm, devouring its soft, molten flesh. They were followed by a pack of ligers that partook in the eating of the worm and also ate the Amelia Bedelias. Like the satyr, the worm bitched about its unfinished, soon-to-be-abbreviated life. The Amelia Bedelias, on the other hand, stubbornly refused to articulate any regrets...

As I continued to observe the narrative of mayhem, a feeling of anxiety and dread paralyzed me. The feeling was unrelated to the digigraffiti. I began to sweat and tremble, but I didn't know why. Something was close. Something was about to happen. Not on the wall, but in real life. I started to hyperventilate.

She appeared. I stopped breathing altogether.

The digigraffiti froze.

She popped up between the bed and the wall as if out of a jack-in-the-box. She made a sharp, horrifying noise that defied representation as she sprang into view.

She was about a foot tall. She was entirely brown and appeared to be made of chocolate. In fact, she looked very much like a chocolate bunny, albeit an emaciated one. A closer inspection revealed she had a human structure. Her hairdo was a tall pointy affair topped off with a bun. Tiny pince-nez sat on the tip of her horned nose. The skin of her face had the texture of a brussel sprout and her lips were knotted into a mad sneer. She wore a little out-of-date buttondown shirt and a shawl over her bowed shoulders. Despite being brown and possibly edible, she looked more like a librarian than a bunny.

It was horrifying.

But I couldn't move. And I couldn't scream.

And I couldn't look away.

My joints left me. My bones turned to iron, my internal organs to brick. Paralyzed, I lay in my bed like a statue that's been pushed onto its side. My body felt so heavy...I began to sink into the mattress. The bunk bed made cracking sounds. Soon it would cave in and crush me. I prayed for it to happen.

The brown lady...She didn't flinch and her expression never changed. She was as harmless as a popsicle on a stick. Yet I had never been so terrified. Tears poured out of my rotund eyes as I stared into the miniature, empty eyes of a monster who I sensed was an incarnation of the Devil. I recalled thinking how it all made sense. My mother-thing experienced demonic possession and had to be exorcised regularly. I figured it was my turn.

Then, suddenly, my body came back to me. The digigraffiti reanimated.

I sprung into a sitting position and cried for my mother-thing, pretending the brown lady wasn't there but eyeing her just the same. The logical thing to do would have been to sprint to my mother-thing's bedcube for refuge. But I stayed in my bed.

My mother-thing didn't come. Eventually my lungs gave out. I stopped calling for her. I turned and faced the brown lady.

I said, "Go, please. Go away, please. Thusly." I didn't know what the latter word meant but my mother-thing always said it when she wanted something. I'm not sure she understood what the word meant either, but I liked saying it. And it assuaged my anxiety. I started to whisper it over and over. "Thusly. Thusly. Thusly. Thusly."

The brown lady stared at me.

I remained in bed. Now I began to whisper-scream for my mother-thing. Unless she was sitting next to me, she wouldn't have been able to hear me. But I whisper-screamed anyway.

...She stumbled into the bedcube.

The thick locks of her hair were fastened in tinfoil, copper wires, scrunchies, curlers and other bindings. Drunk and confused, she walked forward as if her knees had been unscrewed, falling into the walls and then bouncing erect. I watched her through a chink in the drop-drawer.

She opened the drop-drawer, tried to crawl inside and hit her head on an overhang. She somersaulted backwards across the bedcube...

The brown lady stared at me.

My mother-thing got up and staggered to the bed again. She climbed on without incident this time, her breasts spilling out of her nightgown. "What's wrong?" she asked. Her breath stunk of Mad Dog.

I pointed at the brown lady.

"Oh."

My mother-thing reached across the bed. One of her breasts spanked my cheek.

Snorting, she gripped the brown lady, pushed her down beneath the bed and gave her a crank, as if locking her into place. "There." She kissed my forehead. She eased me into my pillow. "Goodnight, son."

As she retreated from the bed, my eyes begged her to stay, but she didn't see me, and then she was gone. I didn't follow her.

I closed my eyes and fell sleep.

The next morning, I couldn't look underneath the bed.

At breakfast I thanked my mother-thing for her assistance and asked why the brown lady was living in my room, how long she had been living there, and why I had never seen her before.

"Goodnight, son," said my mother-thing, and passed out. The plate of soggy eggs and raw bacon she had been holding flew out of her hand and shattered against the ceiling...

I started sleeping on the top bunk, buried in a hill of toys and unable to turn onto my side under any circumstance. To this day I still can't do it. The only position anybody will ever find me in a bed is on my back.

A few weeks later I found the courage to take a peek beneath my lower bunk. Nothing was there, of course.

I became a light sleeper. I woke up all the time in the middle of the night, even when I muted the digigrafitti. The slightest disturbance or vibration beckoned my consciousness. Sometimes my heartbeat was enough to rouse me. Once I woke from the sound of an ant stomping across the carpet of my bedcube.

The brown lady never returned. On occasion, however, I could see her silhouette in my periphery, lingering at my bedside...

18
battle royal – 3rd person

Student-thing Happy Q. Squarebone was late again. He had been seeing his third string sorority girl's 'gänger on the sly. Nothing got him off in bed like a good old-fashioned dirty mouth, and the android's mouth was much dirtier than its owner's. Sometimes he insisted that it actually eat dirt before sleeping with him. He liked to feed it a particular brand: Mr. Greenjeans' Saleté Noire. He kept a big plastic bag of it underneath his bed. Whenever he got the itch, he hauled the bag out, dumped some onto a plate, arranged it into three sections (each representing a different serving of food), gave the 'gänger a fork, and ordered it to dine.

Today he fed the 'gänger too large a portion. It choked and died. He and a group of fratboys who had been observing the meal disposed of the body by carving it into thin slices and feeding it to an industrial paper shredder. The project took longer than expected. Now St. Squarebone faced another tardy point in his ENG 350CC (Novels Concerning Bullfrogs) course. He couldn't afford the point. His professor was a reasonable and fair plaquedemic, but he had been tardy on five occasions this semester. He didn't know the university had been shut down for the day because of a holocaust. As far as he knew, one more tardy ensured his death.

He wasn't tardy yet, though. Class didn't officially begin for twelve minutes. Corndog University's building was twenty blocks ahead. He couldn't make it there on time by foot. But a jetpack would suffice...

He kidney-punched an unsuspecting alaristrian who was bending over to

169

tie his shoe. Gasping, the alaristrian fell forward. The student-thing clocked him in the back of the head with his bookbag, then kicked a hole in his face and stripped him of his jetpack.

The eggs of his brains gurgled onto the asphalt.

The streets, slideways and escalators were crowded, but nobody seemed to notice the crime. St. Squarebone strapped on the jetpack, secured his bookbag and prepared to lift off.

He felt the hairs on his neck singe...He got sucked backward off his feet... then projected forward in a flaming, airborn somersault...He crashed through the window of a cucumber café. The burlap arm of his jumpsuit was on fire. He thrust it into a pot of cucumber soup. The cashier screamed. The lights flashed on and off. St. Squarebone felt himself up. No broken bones. But he was bleeding, gouged, burnt...dizzy...He staggered to the window and peered outside.

Smoke billowing into a nightcrawler sky...Stampede of bodies aflame, bawling and flailing...In an above flyway, alaristrians crashed into each other, spun out of control and exploded...Across the street, a burning beast. The flames crackled and fumed. Smell of overcooked Spaghetti-Os...

Explosion...the flames rose in sweltering umbrellas...Implosion. The aircraft tried to stand up...It slumped over with a defeated groan. Sparks, electric ringlets. The dark fog of a dead thing...

Disoriented, the major domo of the cucumber café accused St. Squarebone of vandalism and insisted he pay for the window he crashed through and the soup he used to put the fire out on his arm.

St. Squarebone lurched outside...

Blast of hot air...His eyes began to bleed. He tripped over a skeleton and fell into the gutter...Faded in and out of consciousness, struggling to keep his vision in focus. Thick walls of smoke encased him.

Abraham Lincoln stepped through the smoke in slow motion...

He looked more like a cartoon than a real person—his skin and clothes luminesced and the contours of his body were uncannily sharp. He was adorned in proverbial Lincolnesque attire—top hat, eyeglasses, bow tie, long suit coat—with the addition of a Frank-N-Furter corset and kneehigh Electra boots. In one hand he carried a ray gun, in the other a chainsword.

"The dogmas of the quiet past are inadequate to the stormy present," he intoned.

Following Lincoln was a meek, hunched-over, Igorlike being who barked, "Quit quoting the President-thing." He exhibited moon boots and a white, loose-fitting swashbuckler shirt that had been ripped and scorched in places. He had a nondescript face in spite of a classic Love-is-a-Battlefield hairdo.

St. Squarebone reached out to them...

Lincoln told the Igor to take cover. The Igor refused. They got into an argument. A flaming skeleton dashed by them. Lincoln clotheslined the skeleton and took off its skull.

Slowly the smoke cleared.

Lincoln and the Igor were still arguing when the army trudged onto the scene.

The army featured vigilantes, ninjas, bounty hunters, Pigs and Cerberus dogs as well as a host of rainforest creatures recruited by the Law to hunt down what the Media was currently calling BBP (Bliptown's Bubonic Plaquepidemic). A troop of Voss Winkenweirder ghosts accompanied the horde. The movie star's family had hired a Ouija diva to summon the ghost and then they had it cloned by a top-of-the-line parageneticist. Needless to say, the ghosts were in vengeful moods. A glittering fog of Papanazi pulsed overhead.

A Pig wearing a Victorian police commissioner's hat put a bullhorn to its snout and announced something in Squealspeak.

The Igor dashed across the street and dove into the cucumber café. He landed head-first in a basket of fresh cucumbers.

Abraham Lincoln said, "If I were to try to read, much less answer, all the attacks made on me, this shop might as well be closed for any other business. I do the very best I know how—the very best I can. And I mean to keep doing so until the end."

The members of the army exchanged confused glances. A Frankenstein monster grunted.

Lincoln shot the Pig-in-Chief with the ray gun. A cobalt radioluminescent aura formed around the Pig. Its body flashed and turned to shadow. The shadow blew away like grains of sand and its big hat fell on the ground.

Bolts of lightning erupted from the Papanazi stormcloud as the army attacked.

St. Squarebone crawled out of the gutter and fell back into the cucumber café. The major domo was reprimanding the Igor now, although when he saw St. Squarebone, he said, "I haven't forgotten about you!"

Lincoln took out the first two lines of blitzkriegers with the ray gun, using the chainsword to repel ammunition fired on him. The third line was a morass of Winkenweirder ghosts. The gun had no effect on the holographic figures. They swarmed him like killer bees, trying to leap into his body and possess it. Lincoln slashed them in pieces with the chainsword. The pieces reformatted and came at him again. He ditched the ray gun. He leapt backwards, somersaulting in fasttime...In the air he pulled a poltergun out of one of the overfull de la Footwas in his pants. The poltergun operated in reverse, inhaling and disintegrating beyond-the-grave life forms.

By the time Lincoln landed on his feet, no ghosts remained...

"St. Squarebone?" the Igor said, pushing the café's major domo aside. He checked his watch. "Why aren't you in class?"

The student-thing was in rough shape. He didn't process the question. Nor did he comprehend that the Igor was his professor for Novels Concerning Bullfrogs.

The major domo clipped the Igor from behind. He fell into a tower of cucumber finger sandwiches. The cashier screamed again.

"Those took me all morning to make!" the major domo shouted.

"You pushed me into them!" The Igor stood up, wiped a glob of mayonnaise from his eye, and slapped the major domo.

An old man sat alone at a table. Unfazed by the commotion, he quietly sipped a cup of exfoliating tea...

A bounty hunter in a Shazam outfit beelined Abraham Lincoln and tried to capture him in a big pillowcase. Lincoln cut his head off with the chainsword. He dropped the head in the pillowcase and swung it at the speed of a helicopter blade, battering the flock of somersaulting ninjas that pounced on him.

He let go of the pillowcase. It flew into the cloud of Media overhead and a handful of Papanazis dropped out of the sky.

"Nearly all men can stand adversity," Lincoln said, "but if you want to test a man's character, give him power." He dropped the chainsword and started to remove weapons from his pockets with machinic proficiency and velocity.

He threw a living torpedo at an abominable snowman. The torpedo was a three-eyed hairless bat. It awoke in mid-air. Screeching, it hit the abominable snowman's hairy chest and chewed out its heart.

He threw a contamination wad at a vigilante. The wad was a fist-sized chunk of slimy flesh. It hit the vigilante's face and a skin disease spread across his body. In seconds his flesh shriveled and dissolved. The vigilante crumpled into a quivering, bloody lump.

He threw a vibronic eel at a vigilante's 'gänger. The eel smacked its neck, wrapped around it and constricted...The 'gänger's head popped off like a bottlecap.

He threw a tanglevine at a King Kong. The weapon looked like a large weed. It hit the giant ape's knee, replicated, and spread across its body until it was completely enveloped. Then the tanglevine compressed back to its original size...A blast of simian blood and viscera showered the army. Two of its soldiers drowned.

He threw a psychoactive spike at a T-Rex. It hit the dinosaur in the temple and incited a hallucination. Suddenly the dinosaur believed it was a coffee pot. It sat down on its tail, squeezed its eyes shut, and tried its best to percolate...

Fusillade of bullets, heat rays, energy bolts, flechettes, shuriken, hypodermics, caltrops, grenades, mortars, throwing stars, fireballs, harpoons, bricks, javelins, rockets, missiles, coral snakes...

Abraham Lincoln leapt into the air, pirouetted, grabbed and spun around a street lamp, jackknifed over a King Kong that tried to bearhug him, and landed on the hood of a blown-up Buick. A velociraptor sprung at him. He caught it by the jaws and ripped its head in two.

Fusillade of bullets, heat rays, energy bolts, flechettes...

Lincoln leapt into the air...

"I'm talking to you young man," the Igor said. "How many tardies do you have this semester?" He started towards the student-thing, who was balled up underneath a spice rack. The café's major domo hit him on the back of the head with a soup spoon.

"Ouch!"

The Igor wrenched the spoon from his grip and wedged the spoon between his legs. The pudgy major domo squealed, grabbed his crotch and tipped over.

The cashier opened a safe in the wall and stared at the barcode inside until she had depleted the café's savings funds. Then she ran out the back door.

"Thief," whimpered the major domo.

The Igor grabbed St. Squarebone's foot and pulled him out into the open. He kicked him in the stomach. "Did you at least do your reading for today? I was going to present a lecture on *The Wind in the Willows* and the theoretical Afterward that accompanies it. Are you prepared to discuss this text? Are you prepared to answer questions in regards to the syllogistic implications of the protagonist's negative capability?"

"Please, Dr...." St. Squarebone had regained his mental faculties. He knew who the Igor was now. But his throat had been burnt to a crisp; when the initial blast from the Smaug crash hit him, he inhaled a tongue of fire. He tried to beg for mercy. "Dr....Dr...."

"Dr. 'Blah. Dr. Blah Blah Blah."

"I'm sorry," the student-thing rasped. "But...the sorority...her 'gänger... She died."

"Your turn." Dr. 'Blah extracted a medieval crusader sword from his pocket.

He hoisted the weapon over his head...and was stabbed in the calf with a fork by the major domo. It was a plastic fork and didn't even puncture the fabric of his pants. But it stung. And it brought back memories.

The major domo became Gilbert Hemingway, Utensil Tyrant. Dr. 'Blah went ballistic. Screeching like a monkey, he swung the sword at the major domo as hard as he could, repeatedly, and missed his target every time. The major domo dodged the blows with ease.

In time Dr. 'Blah destroyed the café. Shards of glassware and cucumber chunks littered the floor, and the dessert carousel lay in ruins. St. Squarebone had retreated beneath the spice rack again. Exhausted, Dr. 'Blah caught his breath, apologized to the major domo, and ordered something cold to drink...

Outside the melee neared a climax. The Papanazi had swelled and expanded into a full-fledged hurricane that spanned blocks and blocks. Winds accelerated up to 80 mph, sweeping humans and 'gängers and Frankenstein monsters off of their feet and throwing the larger rainforest creatures into buildings. Dinosaurs roared and cracked their tails. King Kongs pounded their chests. Abominable snowmen and sasquatches tore their hair out. Lightning drilled the street. Abraham Lincoln hovered between heaven and earth on the thrusters of a Beetlesneak jetpack. The sky shone around him like a million suns, calling him on and on across the universe...

His body slipped into the Bizarro dimension of fasttime. Armed only with a hypersharp rapier, he annihilated the minions of the postcapitalist confederacy...The scene kicked off with a slashed jugular. Before the jugular bled dry, the scene had evolved into a histrionic spectacle of bouncing heads, twitching limbs, spurting gashes and intestinal fireworks...An unsuspecting Pig's snout was hacked off and blue blood gushed out of the hole...An allosaurus' stomach was slashed from the neck to the anus. Its skin opened up like a body bag and out dumped half a ton of whale blubber...D.C. Comics superheroes and villains diced into precise cubes of beef fondue...bouquets of blood and flesh-confetti...soaking technologies...sledgehammer of sparks...thunder, lightning... smell of cooked meat...exploding eyeballs...exploding light bulbs...exploding windows and demolished brick walls...Barbarella yawps...whirlwinds of dark ninja hoods and gees...hairdos tousling into anonymity...rumble of thunder... rhizome of lightning...black-and-white flashbulbs of digitized ultraviolence... close-up on Lincoln's sharp, bearded visage and the purposeful gleam in his bright...white...irisless eyes...

The major domo attempted to chew off Dr. 'Blah's ear. Dr. 'Blah elbowed him in the stomach and punched him in the nose, breaking it. The major domo staggered backwards. Focusing, Dr. 'Blah swung at him with the heavy sword in a 360 degree circle.

He made contact. The major domo fell into two spurting halves.

The old man finished his exfoliating tea, dabbed the corners of his mouth with a handkerchief, and toppled onto the floor, dead of natural causes.

St. Squarebone reeled out of the café. He tripped and fell into the gutter again. Bones sprung into the air. A stream of blood and viscera doused him. He gagged, vomited. He pushed himself out of the carnage.

For a moment he thought he had died and gone to Hell. The street was on fire. The sky was a blizzard of electric insects. Corpses of humans everywhere. Corpses of androids everywhere. Corpses of fictional and extinct beasts everywhere.

"St. Squarebone!"

Moaning, the student-thing staggered down the flaming street. Dr. 'Blah ordered him to stop. He kept going.

Dr. 'Blah squinted, breathed...He cocked the sword and hurled it.

It slammed into the student-thing's back. Blood sprayed out of St. Squarebone's mouth as he wheeled onto his face and snapped his neck.

Abraham Lincoln joined Dr. 'Blah outside the cucumber café. They looked at each other and walked over to St. Squarebone. The boy was dead. The President-thing put his hand on the plaquedemic's shoulder.

"Nice to see you join in the fight," Dr. Identity said, tearing off its mask.

Dr. 'Blah stared down at the corpse. "Too many tardies."

19
death of a salesman – 1st person (identity)

He once told me about the day he purchased me...

The door-to-door salesman was a replica of Willy Loman as portrayed by the actor Dustin Hoffman in the 1985 film version of Arthur Miller's play. When he opened the door he wondered if the disguise was intentional or coincidental. Did the salesman know he was a plaquedemic? Did he know he was a plaquedemic of a particular brand? Did he know he was a plaquedemic of a particular brand who would recognize a replica of Willy Loman as portrayed by the actor Dustin Hoffman in the film version of Arthur Miller's play when he saw one? What were the chances? Was somebody he knew lurking beneath the disguise? Was it even a disguise? Perhaps this was Dustin Hoffman's great-great-great-etc.-grandson. But what were the chances of the grandson looking exactly like his great-great-great-etc.-grandfather? And what were the chances of him dressing up like a character that his great-great-great-etc.-grandfather played in a film? And what were the chances that his real life profession was the same profession owned by the character in his fictional life?

"Can I help you?" the plaquedemic asked.

"No," said the Loman. He smiled. "But I can help you, sir." He looked down at the guitar case in his grasp. It was bigger than him. "Do you want my help?"

"Not really."

"Okay. Bye." He made no effort to leave.

They stared at each other for half a minute. "Wait. Come in."

"Thank you." The salesman stepped inside.

The plaquedemic looked the salesman up and down. "I didn't know door-to-door salesmen still existed."

"How do you know I'm a door-to-door salesman?"

"There's a sign on your hat that says so." He pointed at it.

"Oh."

"So you still exist, I guess."

"I do. But it's a secret. Don't tell anybody."

The plaquedemic gnawed introspectively on a pinky finger. "Do I know you?"

"I don't think so. Maybe. Certainly. But maybe not. I'm certain the answer is maybe not."

"What are you, Willy Loman?"

"Willy Loman?"

"What's going on out there?" yelled the plaquedemic's wife-thing from the kitchenette.

"Nothing!"

He told the salesman they would have to forgo trivialities. "Sell me something. Try anyway. I'm broke." He disliked salesmen. He disliked the very idea of salesmen and probably wouldn't buy anything on that condition alone. But confrontation wasn't his specialty. And he had an overactive sense of empathy. He knew the salesman's pain. He would have felt too guilty if he sent him away without giving him a chance. Yet he deeply resented the salesman for invading his life and tampering with his emotional spectrum. He wanted to hug him. He wanted to strangle him.

The salesman bowed. "I understand. Trivialities, however, are the game's name. I'm sorry." He pushed his way passed the plaquedemic and glided into the kitchenette where the wife-thing was petting and doting over a Bundt cake. She shrieked at the sight of the stranger and dropped the cake on the floor. She accused him of frightening her. But she was quickly won over by his humorous dialogue. The salesman took her hand and stroked it. He asked her name and said it was very pretty. She blushed. He eased her onto the dining table, removed her apron, slipped off her panties and unzipped his trousers.

He stuck his cock in her hole...

The plaquedemic waited patiently for them to finish in the doorway of the kitchenette. A few times he asked, "Are you finished yet?" The wife-thing ignored him. The salesman dutifully replied, "One moment, please."

Afterwards the men retired to the living cube loveseat. The salesman cleared off a coffee table and set his guitar case atop it. He patted the case. "Inside is the answer."

"The answer?"

"That's correct."

"What answer?"

"*The* answer?"

"To what?"

"*It.*"

Their voices were dim. But I could hear them talking...

The salesman explained that he could piece me together in several minutes. Then it was simply a matter of filling out a questionnaire and jacking the plaquedemic's psyche into mine for programming. The process was psychosomatic. My mind would be formatted according to the technology of his desire→→→→and then so would my body. "You can create anything," the salesman assured him, "as long as you understand that, whatever it is, its actions will belong to you by signed contract." He asked the salesman if that was really true. The salesman said, "No. Not really. The fact is you can't create anything. There are certain existential rules and regulations that must be taken into consideration. And it has to look exactly like you. If you want it to look differently, you have to alter your own image first. The rest of what I said is true, though. Mostly."

The plaquedemic expressed some concern about price. The salesman squeezed his knee and assured him I was perfectly affordable. Even if I wasn't affordable it would be a tragedy not to buy me.

"Tragedy?" he said.

"When the feeling's gone and you can't go on," said the salesman.

"I'm broke."

"Nobody's broke."

"Everybody's broke."

"Are you sure? Can you prove it in a court of Law?"

"Nobody can prove anything in a court of Law."

"Indeed."

The plaquedemic couldn't say no. The salesman lifted a finger. Implanted into the tip of it was a small yellow smiley face wearing mirrorshades. He told his customer to grimace for the camera.

Five seconds later the plaquedemic's debt transcended comprehension. But there was a chance the debt would be paid off in only two generations if his children and his children's children worked hard enough. A third generation might be necessary. He had been reticent to have kids despite the wife-thing's constant pleading and crying about being childless. This afternoon they would have a talk about making her a young mother-thing.

The salesman opened the guitar case and removed me. In my protolithic form I resembled something like a giant walking stick or deathly anorexic marionette puppet. I couldn't feel anything. But I was aware of my body. My mind was schizofunctional.

The plaquedemic filled out the questionnaire. The salesman liquefied his responses and blended them in a Petri dish with a sample of his blood and two special ingredients called Badass and the McGuyver Factor. He sprinkled a bit of table salt on top. He sucked up the resultant mixture with an antique-looking syringe and injected the mixture into one of my extremities. Finally he put a straw into a hole in my shriveled head.

"Blow. Hard."

The wife-thing peeked into the living cube. "Can I interest either of you gentlemen in a piece of cake? I picked it up from the floor. I dusted it off. I put it on the table. It's sitting there now. Good as new!"

"Woman!" the salesman snarled. "Goddamn your cake and bring us thirsty bulls a couple of scotches!"

"But, but."

"Do as I say!"

The wife-thing hurried back into the kitchenette. She tried to hide in the refrigerator. Not enough room. She wrapped herself in the tablecloth. She locked her knees. She tipped over into the wall and froze there pretending to be a patio umbrella.

The salesman touched the plaquedemic's thigh. "I'm sorry about that. It's awkward when customers have to see their wife-things reprimanded. But we've all got jobs to do, isn't that so? Blow now."

My head flopped closer to the plaquedemic. "The fragrance is the color of a scream," I said.

"It spoke!"

"Yes. Sometimes it speaks. That's what happens. You better get moving. Without the user's Breath of Life, the machine may acquire down syndrome, or hermaphroditism, or cerebral palsy, or webbed toes, or an allergic reaction to aardvarks, or some such birth defect. I've seen neglected 'gängers come to life that were anthropomorphous globs of noses. Granted, some of the noses were extremely good-looking and went on to become supermodels for clip-on mustaches and pince-nez, but as a whole the 'gänger they comprised was reliably malcontent and couldn't function without its medication."

"I get the picture." The plaquedemic filled his lungs with air. He wrapped his lips around the straw and blew until his cheeks turned purple...

He gasped for air as I sprung across the living cube and crashed into a clock face. Ticks and tocks rained onto my shoulders in slowtime...

My withered limbs swelled and erupted in spasms. An electric current shattered my frail skeleton. My shrunken head melted and a new head crawled out of the residual hole.

I screamed. I screamed.

I heard somebody else scream. I still couldn't see...A bolt of television static struck my visual screen. I grabbed the bolt. My hand caught on fire. My flesh melted. My bones melted...and burned and burned into chrome...My blood sizzled...I screamed. I screamed...Then I could see.

In the beginning was the Image...Later was the Word. Suddenly I possessed a fully loaded WCOED (Wang Chung Oxford English Dictionary) lexicon including unconscious how-to instructions. I discharged a creative magazine of curse words as my body continued the agonizing hustle and flow of inflating and deflating and constructing and reconstructing...

"I'm naked," I said when it was over. I sat by myself on the loveseat. Ectoplasm seeped from my pores and dripped down my skin in large brown chunks. "I shit myself." It was true. I was mired in a pool of feces. I glanced across the room at my original. He was plastered against a wall. "May I have a shower?"

The plaquedemic pinched his nose with his fingers and gawked at the salesman. The salesman stood at attention on the other side of the living cube. He had applied a giant clothespin to his nose.

"I forgot to mention this bit of unpleasantness," he said. "It's worth it, though, don't you think? Sir, meet your match. Literally. Well, not quite literally. Literally in terms of the generally understood connotation of the phrase 'meet your match,' I mean. Does that make sense?"

My original and I looked at each other. I stood up and bowed deeply. He said, "I..."

"Woman!" blurted the salesman. "Get your canned ham out here and clean up this mess! Jesus!" The salesman crossed his arms over his chest. The wife-thing scampered out of the kitchenette at top speed and smashed into a china cabinet. She was still tangled in the tablecloth. She wriggled out of it and got to her feet. She saluted the salesman and began to pick up the broken cups and saucers and dishes.

The salesman yelled, "Leave the china! Tend to the android!"

"Oh!" exclaimed the wife-thing. She broke into tears.

The plaquedemic stepped forward. "Mr. Loman!"

"Loman?" said the salesman. He furrowed his brow.

The plaquedemic picked up a book and threw it at him. The salesman ducked...and climbed onto the plaquedemic's back. He wrapped his legs around his waist and massaged his shoulders and spine. "Calm down now," he said. "It's going to be all right. Sometimes a man has to take control of a situation. You understand. Yes. There you are. My my, you're a bundle of knots. My my. I'll take care of you. How does that feel?"

The plaquedemic closed his eyes and moaned in pleasure.

The wife-thing sprayed me down with a bottle of Windex. Bit by bit she squeaked my body clean. Afterwards she tried to strap me into a diaper. I asked if I could have a pair of Dudley Horrorshow boxer briefs instead. She told me my original couldn't afford that brand of underwear.

"Alas," I said.

The massage felt so good that the plaquedemic fell asleep standing up.

The salesman quietly climbed off of him. He picked up the wife-thing and packed her into the guitar case. He nodded at me. "Good luck then." As he was about to leave the plaquedemic snorted awake and asked where he was going.

The salesman frowned. "Going? Ah yes, going. I'm going home, I suppose. It's almost dinnertime."

"Ahem," said the plaquedemic.

"Oh yes. I almost forgot." He unsnapped the guitar case. The wife-thing rolled out of it. She hit the floor and shrieked. "Well then," the salesman said. "I guess that's it. I'd like to take this opportunity to say that I appreciate your business. Have a nice day then. Bye." He slammed the door shut behind him.

My original placed his fists on his hips and frowned at me...

Later that night the salesman died in his sleep. The obituary said he was 54 years old. Forensic schizoanalysts determined that at the time of death he had been dreaming about butlers. The butlers were jetpacking across the troposphere in a great V-shape. Each carried a plate of hors d'oeuvres and wore astronaut bubbles on their heads in case they slipped out of formation and fell into space.

According to the coroner the cause of death was the fear of dying alone.

20
barracuda vs. bogue – 3ʳᵈ person

The debate ran simultaneously on over twenty thousand channels. Disting-uished Congressman-thing Chapman Barracuda was squaring off against incumbent President-thing Grimley Bogue, leader of the Pogocratic party and the science fictionalized world. A member of the Headless Horseman party, Congressman-thing Barracuda was in the middle of critiquing the current administration's advocacy of a particular brand of hairdo called The Dirty Figaro, an unorthodox piece infamous for inciting the belief in its users that they were messiahs. Some people bought it just to see if they could fend off the belief. Invariably they failed. "And that's precisely the point," the congressman-thing tooted.

"Fuck that point," the President-thing broke in, hopping in place on his proverbial pogo stick. "That point doesn't make any sense. You're such a cunt."

The mouth of the congressman-thing's jack-o-lantern shriveled into a prune. "Cunt?" He clutched his chest and staggered backwards. "How dare you call me a cunt on national television! How dare you, sir!"

"I'll call you whatever I want on national television! I'm the President-thing." Exhibiting supernatural dexterity, he spread out his arms and bowed for the camera while still managing to hop up and down on the pogo stick.

Three volcanic seconds of applause superimposed a laugh track...

Congressman-thing Barracuda gestured at somebody off-camera. "This isn't fair! I'm trying to have a civilized debate and he's calling me names! What the hell is going on here?"

"Quit being such a baby. You sound like my grandkid for Chrissakes. Address the issue on the table or get the rotten fuck out of my kitchen."

Congressman-thing Barracuda removed his jack-o-lantern. Beneath it was a dirty, rotting skull. Closer inspection revealed it to be a skull-shaped vegetable that appeared to have just been yanked out of the soil. More than a few children watching the broadcast buried their faces between their mother-thing's breasts, scared of the politician.

The congressman-thing lifted the jack-o-lantern over his head and smashed it on the stage in a fit of anger.

President-thing Bogue said, "Let me know when your temper tantrum is over. In the meantime I'd like to have a personal conversation with the Amerikan people. Can you hear me Amerika?" He smiled at the camera.

Hysterical, Congressman-thing Barracuda attacked the President-thing. He dashed across the stage and tried to tackle him. The President-thing hopped over him. The congressman-thing crashed into an urn of flagpoles. He picked one up and tossed it at the President-thing like a javelin. The President-thing bounced out of the way. He picked up another flagpole and charged the President-thing, shrieking at an ear-splitting pitch. He slipped on a piece of pumpkin. His legs flew over his head and he landed on his back. His head smacked against the floor and cracked open. The camera zoomed in→ → → →to the wound...

"My skull!" howled Congressman-thing Barracuda. "My spine! I'm broken!"

President-thing Bogue regarded his opponent grimly.

Papanazi swarmed the stage. They galloped and jetpacked over to the injured congressman-thing and devoured the image of his grotesquerie. Livid, the President-thing pulled two Colt six-shooters out of holsters in his Texarkana suit. The handguns contained internal microwombs that virginbirthed new bullets the instant an adult bullet was discharged, rendering infinite supplies of ammunition. The President-thing was an expert marksman and unloaded over a hundred rounds in seconds. He wounded and killed most of the Papanazi and scared the rest away.

He blew smoke from the tips of the Colts and flipped them back into their holsters. He hopped across the stage, tripping over corpses but never losing his balance. "Get a doctor! No contender for President-thing's gonna die in my presence! That's shitty karma! Medic!"

Diminutive men and 'gängers wearing bleached white jackets and stethoscopes crawled onto the stage. They waddled towards Congressman-thing Barracuda as the camera cut to a commercial.

The commercial advertised a new variety of Dr. Identity action figure. Unlike former models, this one came equipped with de la Footwa pockets containing endless, fully operable supplies of classic science fiction weapons. It was sentient, too, and included a large supply of facemasks and personalities, ersatz veins coursing with Hammer blood, a chameleon skinsuit and flippers, four refills of Hammer blood, a token Dr. 'Blah sidekick (non-sentient), and, for added effect, a vintage *Star Wars* jawa. Viewers were warned that the action figure would only be available for a limited time. Very likely it would be taken off the market in no time at all.

The next commercial advertised an upgraded version of the new variety of Dr. Identity action figure advertised in the preceding commercial. The upgrade was outfitted exactly like its predecessor with one twist: it possessed superhuman babysitting skills.

The next commercial advertised an old brand of Dr. Identity cereal with a new image of the upgraded version of the new variety of Dr. Identity action figure on the box cover. An actor's 'gänger (or an actor disguised as a 'gänger) dressed like Dr. Identity poured the cereal into a large bowl, poured milk over the cereal, and set the bowl on a table. The action figure then swung onto the table from off-camera and attacked the bowl with an electroshock mace...

Seven more commercials followed. The first six were repeats of the first three commercials two times over. The last one announced the impending death of all Dr. Identity products, especially action figures and cereal. Nothing could last forever, and marketing conglomerates were running out of ideas. In order to deal with the loss, sponsors urged consumers to seek out their local witch doctors and exorcists for assistance in coming to terms with the illusory feelings of demonic possession that might ensue.

A global earthquake accompanied the consumer bombardment of every Littleoldladyville in the Amerikanized universe...A cosmology of television screens turned to static and white noise. The holocaust was quickly replaced by the Technicolors of the spectrum and a quiet, hypnotic whistle. Then:

"And now we return to our regularly scheduled program."

Congressman-thing Barracuda was propped up in a wheelchair, a fresh jack-o-lantern wedged onto his head. Barely discernable facial features had been haphazardly carved onto its surface, and its insides weren't fully hollowed out: seeds and pulp oozed down the congressman-thing's chest and shoulders.

Grimley Bogue stood next to him, a hand resting on his shoulder. He climbed back onto his pogo stick when he noticed the camera had turned back on. The congressman-thing tipped into his lap. The President-thing got off the pogo stick and propped him up again. He wrapped a length of wire tubing around his chest and the back of the wheelchair to make sure he stayed in place, then climbed back onto the pogo stick. He gained altitude with each playful hop.

"Right! Next question!"

The moderator of the debate rose from his chair. The camera zoomed in→→→→on his bald spot, held for a beat, and zoomed back out.

"Thank you, Mr. President-thing," said the moderator. "The next question concerns the latest edition of Yahtzee. How do you feel about the addition of a ten-sided Dungeons & Dragons die to the board game? Let's start with Congressman-thing Barracuda."

"I'm first!" barked the President-thing.

"Okay," said the moderator.

"Hrrrrrm," said Congressman-thing Barracuda. A glob of pulp spilled out of his deformed grin.

The President-thing reached such a height that he started to disappear into the top of the camera frame.

The moderator cleared his throat. "Yes, sir. Of course. Your response?"

"That's a dumbass question!" he shouted from the rafters. "Try again!"

Cursing the pogocratic party beneath his breath, the moderator nervously shuffled through a stack of note cards. Pogocratics were notorious for on-camera incorrigibility, trouble-making and lewd behavior. Yet the Amerikan people had nominated one as their President-thing in spite of the scores of specialized political parties that now existed within the government. Remnants of the once dominant Democratic and Republican parties still survived, although they held virtually no power and their representatives never got elected for influential positions. Their representatives mainly acted as clerical subordinates for more dynamic parties. According to the *National Kaptain's Log*, the most dynamic party currently in existence was the Parsley Garnishers, whose members' ideology prescribed parsley as a holy weed that should only be used as a garnish under extreme dining circumstances. In second place was the Headless Horseman party due to a curious resurgence of public interest in the Disney adaptation of Washington Irving's *The Legend of Sleepy Hollow*. Then there were the Gitchy Goomers, gleefully brainwashed by the persistent mass appeal of the Neil Diamond ballad...the Ku Klux Kahn, known for their smoothly shaven, oversized pectoral muscles and acidic catch phrases patterned after the arch-villain of the archetypal *Star Trek II*...Kra-takka-takka-takka-tams, their name a piece of onomatopoeia used in various comics books to denote the crumbling noise of a falling wall. It was this party's frequent practice during governmental assemblies to construct tall, seemingly sturdy sand castles and then knock them down so that they could articulate the sound of their party name....Pogocratics currently held the twenty-fifth ranking. Other than keeping pogo sticks as party insignia, they were nihilists and had no ideological affinity with the vehicles. Generally speaking, they were hated, ridiculed, and assassinated on a regular basis. But Grimely Bogue had struck a chord with the Amerikan people in the last election. He happened to be bouncing down a slidewalk to the senate house one morning when a terrorist attack broke out in a nearby turtle store. The terrorists had subdued the 'gängers running the place, set all of the artificial turtles free, dragged all of the real turtles out into the street and systematically lit them on fire, claiming they were abominations. The Papanazi flooded the scene and Bogue immediately leapt at the opportunity to "do some cunt-licking good," as he later admitted in a State-of-the-Union address. There were three terrorists, but Bogue made quick work of them. Gaining speed and height, he vaulted into the air and came down on the do-badders like a hammer, nailing them into the concrete. And afterwards he tended to the wounded turtles until the Pigs showed up. He became a national icon, and despite the unspeakable villainy he had committed before and after that moment as an elected official and private citizen, soon he was slouching in the Highchair of the Off-White House's Opaque Office...

Eight seconds passed and the moderator still hadn't selected an alternate question. The President-thing reduced his altitude until he merely bobbed up and down. "Hurry up you worthless pimp! The Amerikan people are watching and waiting!"

The camera did a 180 degree revolution→↑←and swung into a close-up of the moderator→→→→The pocks on his ruddy cheeks showed beneath his makeup. Beads of sweat trickled down his forehead. His lower lip had disappeared behind an upper row of horse teeth. "Go away," he whispered to the camera. The camera giggled and reverted to its original position.

"Ask me a question!"

"Uhm. Uhm."

"Ask me a question shitforbrains!"

The moderator closed his eyes and pulled out a random note card. He cleared his throat again.

"Quit clearing your throat!"

The moderator apologized and said, "Recent developments in the Mayberry sector of the northeastern rainforest indicate that a group of abominable snowmen have formed a civilized community, complete with church-going and soda-drinking. Firstly, how do you account for this formation? Secondly, what steps are you prepared to take in order to restore disorder? Thirdly—"

"Horseshit!" interrupted the President-thing. He lifted his arm and made a fist. The fist sprung twenty feet from his wrist on a bungee cord, cracked the moderator in the nose, and bungeed back into his wrist. The moderator toppled backwards out of his chair, note cards flying everywhere. "Wrong question!"

Congressman-thing Barracuda gurgled something about "company policy." President-thing Bogue slapped him in the back of the pumpkin.

Quickly the moderator picked up the note cards, turned over the chair and crawled back into it. He got dizzy and fell backwards again. And again he picked up the note cards, turned over the chair and crawled back into it.

And again he got dizzy...

The moderator fell out of his chair five times. As he struggled to stay conscious and upright, the President-thing did a dirty stand-up routine.

Finally the moderator collected himself. He waited for the President-thing to hit his final punch line, then said, "Mr. President-thing sir. You're doubtless familiar with the recent string of serial holocausts in Bliptown committed by two plaquedemics who need no introduction. Dr. Identity and its original have yet to be apprehended. They continue to hunt the streets, flyways and rooftops of Bliptown without receiving so much as a scratch, it seems. Critics have argued that they are either vampires or intelligent zombies—undead at any rate. Do you agree with this contention? If so, what are you prepared to do about them? If not, how do you account for the absurdity of the plaquedemics' relentless existence?"

This time President-thing Bogue allowed the moderator to finish his question. But he was clearly upset by it, so much so that he got off his pogo stick and threw it aside. "Are you finished?" he said.

The moderator nodded doubtfully.

"These are the questions you choose to ask me in front of the entire nation? Christ all goddamn mighty. I am *soooo* sick of hearing about those goddamn plaquedemics. I could care less about those fucking retards. *Nobody* cares about them anymore. Even the Papanazi are bored. Fuck 'em. They've had their fifteen minutes. Their time is up. I declare it. They can commit all of the stinking holocausts they want as far as I'm concerned. It is my decree that from here to eternity the plaquedemics are to be ignored by everybody in spite of the extreme nature of their ultraviolent antics. Failure to ignore them will result in senseless, excruciating torture followed by the surgical removal of the guilty parties' arms and legs from their bodies. Citizens will allow themselves to be murdered or pay the penalty. Citizens will not even speak the plaquedemics' names aloud. I'll write the bill this evening, I'll pass the law in the morning, and I'll deploy the absolute power of the Amerikan military to execute my bidding. The military will start by liquidating all plaquedemic-related tabloid media. This may require burning Bliptown to the ground—for starters. At any rate, fuck those shitheads. Their assholish behavior will come out in the wash with everything else. End response." Unnerved, the President-thing thrust his hands into the pockets of his pants and made low growling noises.

The moderator turned to his opponent. "Congressman-thing Barracuda—your, uh, rebuttal?

"He doesn't have shit to say," said the President-thing, and kicked over the wheelchair he was sitting in. The force of the kick sent the congressman-thing halfway across the stage on his stomach. His jack-o-lantern came off the stump of his head and rolled away...

"This debate is over. Goodnight Amerika."

President-thing Bogue picked up his pogo stick. Holding it like a baseball bat, he leapt off of the stage and began to beat the moderator as the camera cut to a commercial.

The commercial advertised a new variety of President-thing Bogue action figure. Unlike former models, this one came equipped with a Congressman-thing Barracuda punching bag and six backup flying fists, among other accessories...

21
papanazi kontrol – 3rd person

Achtung 66.799 took cover in a newspaper booth. He had to remove a few stacks of newspapers to fit inside, but his body was small enough that he could squat there comfortably. He could almost stand up.

It was a classical Gothic sector. Most of the pedestrians that stumbled up and down the decayed cobblestone street were dressed as monks, vampires, Mr. Hydes, Young Goodman Browns and Phantoms of the Opera. Wooden trap doors had been built into the street. Figures fell in and popped out like gophers. Countless stone gargoyles crouched on the ledges of sharp, black buildings ornamented with stained glass windows. Some of the gargoyles were alive and flew from rooftop to rooftop. Occasionally one swooped down and snatched a baby out of a handmaiden's arms.

According to the Papanazi's sources, there had been an exodus of movie stars to this sector earlier that morning. Armstrong Sarks, Dick Doily, Voss Winkenweirder and Hagar Parakeet were rumored to be among them. The reason for the exodus? Nobody knew for certain, but Achtung 66.799 suspected it had something to do with a Hunchback of Notre Dame fetish that had been afflicting certain celebrity factions lately. He kept a special watch for passersby who had strapped bowling balls to their shoulderblades.

Achtung 66.799 received the tip at 5 a.m. and had been staking out the scene for over two hours now. So far the gig was a bust. At one point he thought he spotted Cinnabar Trait, Carmina Burana Award nominee for a recent BBB-film in which he played the main character's shadow. The man lacked a disguise, but the streetlights were dim and Achtung 66.799 couldn't tell if it was Trait. And when he crawled out of the newspaper stand and accosted the man, he realized it wasn't a man at all, but a shadow...

The Papanazi returned to his hideout. Frustrated, he curled up and fell asleep.

A siege of tickling awakened him. Somebody had opened the chute of the newspaper booth and was fumbling inside. Achtung 66.799 excused himself and climbed out. The 'gänger outside had on a shiny black top hat and cape with puffed up shoulders. He glared disapprovingly at the Papanazi, claimed a newspaper, and marched away.

Yawning, Achtung 66.799 surveyed the area. It was light out and the streets were empty now. His stomach growled. He needed a money shot badly. Once he forged a money shot, trying to pass off a photo of a bag lady stealing a hood ornament as a celebrity. His superiors caught him red-handed and cryogenically froze him in a Papanazi penal colony for three years. Right now he would have willingly forged again—at least you have dreams and receive proper nourishment in the Freeze—but a second offense would result in termination of employment and banishment to the rainforests. This, of course, was contingent upon him getting caught. But the proficiency of the Papanazi's surveillance technology overshadowed that of any other Amerikan social institution, including the Government. Everybody always got caught.

Standard issue depression set in. He was depressed because of his job. He was depressed because of society. He was depressed because his mother-thing didn't love him. He was depressed because he never found a wife-thing to replace her. He was depressed because, even if he found a wife-thing, he couldn't afford to support her. He was depressed because he was undereducated. He was depressed because he was hungry. He was depressed because he was depressed. He was depressed because he was depressed because he was depressed. He was depressed because, if he wasn't depressed, he might miss being depressed, depression being such an essential component of his psychic framework...

He snapped out of it when the signal hit him. Veins of electricity played across the field of jacks on his scalp. The jacks came to life and started arguing with each other. Achtung 66.799 shoved his fingers in his ears and concentrated on the message.

All Papanazi currently not engaged in head-to-head combat needed to report to the nearest Kontrol Center for immediate debriefing on a new story. No information on the story dispatched other than the news of Voss Winkenweirder's murder and the movie star's 'gänger's subsequent meltdown.

Papanazi Kontrol Centers could be found on practically every vertical and horizontal block in Bliptown. Papanazi workerbees like him weren't allowed inside barring rare invitations such as this one. Standard issue euphoria set in now. If nothing else, the Kontrol Centers were loaded with free hors d'oeuvres...

He sprinted down the street, searching left, right, left, overhead...A trap door flung open and swallowed him. He fell into a long, tall passageway reconstructed to look like a nineteenth century Parisian arcade...Lattice of iron girders, catwalks, glass shop windows, gaslight lanterns, tall artificial plants. Flâneurs and stilt-walkers everywhere...Achtung 66.799 whizzed through the underground commerce, searching, searching...He found a Kontrol Center at the end of the passageway.

He wasn't the first workerbee to find it. Scores had preceded him, and they were battling for the hors d'oeuvres. Featured today: shriveled meatballs and dried up celery sticks.

Achtung 66.799 burst through the front door and dove into the mix...

Every Papanazi for himself. Karate chops and roundhouse kicks and flying elbows slammed into faces and stomachs and spines. Sound of cracking bones and heated warcries...

"ACHTUNG!!!"

A strike of lightning followed the directive, emanating from a static-electricity disco ball in the ceiling. It temporarily zombified the Papanazis. Their shoulders slouched. Their mouths dropped open. Fistfuls of meatballs and celery sticks fell to the floor.

"ACHTUNG!!!"

Another lightning bolt. The Papanazis fell into formation, scurrying into a line, thrusting out their chests, turning into statues.

The Sergeant General wafted down the rank on a driftdisc and inspected the troops. Most of them wore SS or Grim Reaper fatigues. Achtung 66.799 had on a cheap Goodbody suit. The Sergeant General stopped in front of him.

"What the fuck is this shit!"

"Sir!"

"Who the fuck do you think you are!"

"Sir!"

"How the fuck do you explain yourself!"

"Sir!"

"What the fuck!"

"Sir!"

"What the fuck!"

"Sir!"

"What the fuck!"

"Sir!"

"What the Fuck!"

"Sir!"

The Sergeant General was a behemoth, seven-foot-tall cyborg. Outsized mechanical hands hung from his bulk like crab claws and he had a giant papier-mâché Joseph Stalin head. His dialect even had a tinge of a Russian accent. He lightly smacked Achtung 66.799 and told him to mind his fashion sense. The blow severely dizzied the Papanazi, but he remained standing in rank. The jacks in his skull, however, were knocked out cold.

Somebody down the line sneezed.

"What the fuck!"

The Sergeant General glided over to the insurgent. His punishment turned out to be stiffer than Achtung 66.799's. Luck of the draw.

"What's your name soldier?" the Sergeant General asked in a decidedly feminine voice.

"Sir! My name is Achtung 446.5—"

The Sergeant General grabbed his head with one great hand and squeezed... The sauce of the soldier's head oozed through the creases of his metal fingers like Play-Dough. He loosened his grip and kicked the corpse in the chest. It sailed end over end across the Kontrol Center into a body basin.

"Anybody else need to sneeze? Anybody have to use the toilet?"

A Papanazi at the end of the rank tentatively raised a hand.

"I admire your honesty," said the Sergeant General. He pulled out an antimatter pistol with an elongated barrel, aimed and fired. The atomic structure of the Papanazi twisted into infinite knots. He melted, molted, congealed, contorted, sparked, flared...Primordial soup was the end of him.

The Sergeant General liquidated two more Papanazi with the antimatter pistol for no reason. He sheathed the weapon. "Enough fun and fucking games. You're here for a reason. Brass tacks."

"Sir!!!"

"At ease then. But stay away from the hors d'oeuvres until we fucking convene."

"At ease" meant the same thing as "achtung" in terms of a soldier's standing position. It just meant a soldier was safe from being murdered by an authority figure.

The Sergeant General quick-drew the antimatter pistol and reduced a Papanazi standing next to Achtung 66.799 to soup.

"I couldn't resist, goddamn it! Pretend I didn't say at ease before. At ease for real now."

Achtung 66.799 flexed his jaw...

The Sergeant General glided to the opposite end of the room. A 3D holoscreen sprouted out of the floor. The heads of a human and his 'gänger dissolved into view and rotated around a central axis like planets around a sun. A code of schematics unfolded beneath them.

"Observe the future of Papanaziism," the Sergeant General said, clicking his heels together. "By future, I mean the next twenty-four hours. Possibly the next twelve hours. Maybe one hour. It all depends on the Media now. It all depends on you now." He slammed his fists together. "These are the perps. They killed Voss Winkenweirder and emotionally incapacitated his 'gänger. They're plaquedemics! They teach English! They've already committed two holocausts this morning. The Law has calculated that they will commit up to eight holocausts by noon. Reasons unknown. Reasons incidental!" He slammed his fists together. "The 'gänger's name is Dr. Identity. It is rumored to possess superheroic strength and scikungfi skills. It stands six feet three inches tall. Its sense of fashion is stable. Its psychological disposition is unstable. It has a distinguishing scar on its forehead. Currently it has no publications under its belt. The human's name is Dr. ———. He is rumored to possess limited strength and scikungfi skills. He stands six feet three inches tall. His sense of fashion is stable. His psychological disposition is unstable. He has no distinguishing scars. Currently he has three publications under his belt. All are literary criticism. His most recent essay, 'The Post(post)/post-post+postmodern Icklyophobe: Ultra/counter\hypernihilism in Fiona Birdwater's Megaanti-micronovel, *The Ypsilanti Factor*,' appears in Issue 2, Volume 6 of an underground, staple-bound journal whose name is irrelevant." *Slam!* "Nicknames for the plaquedemics currently include the Dystopian Duo, Team Hatewave, Warlords of Wickedness, the Dawgs of Plaquedemia, and Bartleby's Fangs. New nicknames are being considered for publication. Submissions should be forwarded to Papanazi headquarters. Payment for publication is a get-out-of-death-free coupon at any Littleoldladyville." *Slam!* "Payment for footage of the plaquedemics, footage of any fucking kind, is full retirement with benefits. This is a code blackhead, gentlemen. The plaquedemics should be treated like red hot movie stars straight out of a Big-Budget, Hackademy Award-winning blockbuster. Bear in mind they prefer the air to the streets. Jetpacks and Stickem suits are highly recommended. Questions?"

A Papanazi raised his hand. The Sergeant General hurled a throwing star at him. It slammed into his forehead. He flew backwards in a snarl of limbs and landed in the body basin like a slam dunk.

The Sergeant General passed through the holoscreen, which disintegrated into the floor behind him. He nodded at the remaining soldiers. "You have your orders, gentlemen. Semper fee-fi-fo-fum...I smell the blood of an everyman." The Sergeant General's driftdisc morphed into a black hole and sucked him into it. Then the black hole imploded with a dull snap.

The Papanazis' chests popped like balloons. Gasping for air, they peered at each other out of the corners of their eyes, watchful, calculating...

They fell on the hors d'oeuvres.

Achtung 66.799 salvaged a meatball, then crawled into a storeroom and signed out a jetpack and Stickem suit with accessories. He was billed a pound of flesh. He was billed another pound of flesh for the cost of the surgery it took to patch him up.

For the first time in his life, Achtung 66.799 felt a sense of hope. He wondered how long it would last.

He wondered if it had already passed...

22
dénouement – 1ˢᵗ person ('blah)

Dr. Identity selected a mid-level rooftop in Chop Suey Square. Day and night it was Bliptown's busiest sector. Trafficways of all forms, genres, creeds and velocities stretched above, below and beyond us...

Baryames Bornagainandagain knelt on the edge of the rooftop with his hands locked behind his head. He oscillated between calling us names and offering us royalties from his better-selling films. Dr. Identity had stalked and kidnapped the movie star with the intention of assassinating him, live, in front of the entire city. The android stood behind the actor, a roaring chainsword brandished over its head. It transmitted its POV onto every skyscreen and vidbuilding in Chop Suey Square.

I stood at a safe distance from the scene, making small talk with the curator of a hot dog stand.

Bornagainandagain said, "I'll give you half of my earnings from *The Robobarista*." His real last name was McDarnit. He changed it after a second comeback from BBB-movieland to semi-mainstream cinema. Since the change he had managed not to slip back into obscurity, although if he did again, he resolved to simply tack an ellipsis onto the end of the alias and leave it at that.

Dr. Identity revved the chainsword.

"Sideshow," grumbled Bornagainandagain.

Dr. Identity rapped its knuckles across the movie star's skull, then offered the following overture, which blasted out of every surroundsound satellite in the immediate vicinity: "Citizens of Bliptown! Behold as I, Dr. Identity, remove yet another cultural artifact from the degraded, devolved museum of postcapitalist life! Before me kneels Baryames Bornagainandagain, star of countless low-grade films, sell-out commercials and plotless pornos, but he was an extra in the Papanazi-acclaimed *Honkies & Catnip*, and Patrick Swayze is his distant relative! His death is a flagrant act of terrorism and inexcusable bastardry. I give it to you!"

Dr. Identity threw out its arms, daring somebody to stop it. Its afro trembled in the wind.

Despite the prevalence of Papanazi, professional vigilantes, bounty hunters and Pigs in the trafficways, nobody responded. A few seconds later my 'gänger lost the signal to the skyscreens and vidbuildings...

"Shit!" Dr. Identity tossed the chainsword aside, yanked tight its glitterglove, pulled a carrot out of its Thriller jacket and snapped into it.

"Can I go now?" Bornagainandagain asked, unlocking his fingers.

Dr. Identity chewed the carrot with Bugs Bunnylike relish. "Fine. Go." It kicked the movie star in the back. Bornagainandagain toppled forward and fell, fell, fell...

Dr. Identity joined me at the hot dog stand. Its pupils had become hallucinogenic swirls.

I said, "You know, you're mixing time periods there. The glove came after the jacket. Jackson didn't start with the glove until after the *Bad* album. And your afro is from *Off the Wall*, before he started playing dress-up and molesting children. Not to mention your facemask. It wasn't an actual skull until he got into his hundreds."

"Since when do you know so much about the King of Pop?" Dr. Identity removed the facemask with the glitterglove and inspected it.

"I know lots of things. I'm a plaquedemic."

"Not anymore."

We fell silent. The hot dog curator glanced back and forth between us, wondering if we were going to buy something. Dr. Identity looked bizarre. It had developed a strange fetish for carrot-eating recently. Overindulgence of beta carotene had turned its eyes a bright orange color.

"At any rate," it said, "there's nothing wrong with exhibiting a little temporal diversity. Fashion plates have been doing it for years."

"Fashion plates?"

"Don't say it." Dr. Identity removed the afro and stuffed it into a de la Footwa. He did the same with the facemask and the glitterglove. He kept the Thriller jacket on. "This is discouraging. I'm sick of being ignored. Nobody gives a shit about us anymore. You should have programmed me to deal more effectively with rejection."

I pointed at a corndog and the curator leapt to the task. "That's what happens when you lay it on too thick. People get a bad taste in their mouths. Then the taste just goes away." We had stopped being pursued long ago. Not only did the Law and the Media grow bored with us, there were too many people impersonating us to bother trying to apprehend the real perpetrators. The passing of President-thing Bogue's law against acknowledging our holocaustic behavior didn't help. Nor did the hottest-selling perfume on the market, Plaquedemic Fringe, laced with the scent of our DNA. Even my credit was operable again: thousands of impersonators had opened up bank accounts in my name and numbers...

I was happy. I still didn't know my real name. But I was happy. Unfortunately the Pigs had sold my wife-thing to a small tribe of Frankenstein monsters who lived in the rainforest outside of Bliptown's nine o'clock gate. But foul play begets foul play.

Dr. Identity was having difficulty coming to terms with being out of the limelight. Every now and then he committed a holocaust or murdered a celebrity, hoping to return to mediatized grandeur. It never worked. Since my 'gänger's original act of ultraviolence, it seemed, everybody was committing holocausts and murdering celebrities. The Law decided that that's the way things had been for years and nothing could be done about it by human intervention or rationalization. "Bliptown will shakedown and shakeout its own riffraff in its own time," the Mayor-thing of the city was quoted as saying. Additionally, the

Amerikan government decided that there was an overpopulation of celebrities and they needed to be brought closer to extinction so as to accentuate their market value and public interest.

"Something to eat?" I asked Dr. Identity.

It shook its head. "I'm too depressed to eat."

I paid for my corndog and took a bite. It tasted good. "There's no need to be depressed. Think about your comic book. That's something to look forward to. You've constructed a very detailed outline already. Now all you have to do is draft it. We may want to rethink your title. We may want to rethink some of its minutia. I'd be glad to provide you with constructive criticism."

Dr. Identity glared at me. "The comic book is mine."

I shrugged. "Fair enough. I've got plans of my own anyway."

"No doubt."

"I've been in touch with a group of investors. I told them I was interested in establishing my own university. There are so few left in Bliptown since you came into vogue and popularized making mincemeat out of university property. Copycats of your work are legion. Some of the investors were hesitant. But I reassured them I knew what I was doing and their contributions would pay off. I'm going to be a Dean. I'm not sure what kind of Dean yet. But a Dean nonetheless. And I'm hand-picking every single plaquedemic that works at my university. No more eccentrics. No more absurdists. No more tumbleweeds."

"I see. What will you call your university?"

"I'm torn. Either Blah Blah Blah State University or the University of Blah Blah Blah. Maybe just 'Blah College."

Dr. Identity's pupils morphed into turning cogs. "You're delusional."

I took another bite of the corndog. "Perhaps. But it's a new world now. One man's delusion is another 'gänger's reality."

That night Dr. Identity and I went to my cubapt. I hadn't been there since the morning of the initial holocaust. Dr. Identity hadn't been there since I purchased him. The cubapt was a theater of war. The walls were blood-stained, the furniture was burnt and ripped apart, and none of the appliances worked except for an old television set, a 1947 Motorola VT105 I had bought at an underground vintage ADW as a graduate student. We lay on the floor and watched the news. Around midnight I told Dr. Identity I was going to bed. The android said goodnight and I turned it off.

About the Author

D. Harlan Wilson is a wannabe Max Headroom impressionist. He also exhibits qualites reminiscent of Dr. Identity and Dr. 'Blah. For more information on Wilson and his work, visit his offical website at www.dharlanwilson.com.

author image courtesy
Brandon Duncan

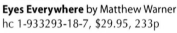

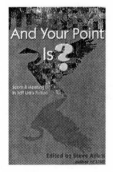

8/09

Printed in the United States
150515LV00006B/131/A

9 781933 293325